AMISH
DILEMMA

A Novel

by

SIOUX DALLAS

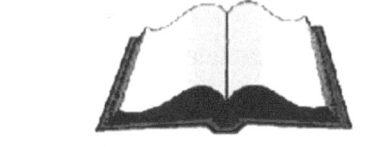

CCB Publishing
British Columbia, Canada

Amish Dilemma: A Novel

Copyright ©2011 by Sioux Dallas
ISBN-13 978-1-926918-67-9
First Edition

Library and Archives Canada Cataloguing in Publication

Dallas, Sioux, 1930-
Amish dilemma : a novel / written by Sioux Dallas. – 1st ed.
ISBN 978-1-926918-67-9
I. Title.
PS3604.A439A75 2011   813'.6   C2011-904338-6

Publisher: CCB Publishing
British Columbia, Canada
www.ccbpublishing.com

Dedicated to my darling daughter, Verta Lynn, for whom I thank God daily. She has a heart as big as all outdoors and takes in and cares for stray animals and sometimes needy people. She is a treasure. I am so blessed. She said she thinks God put her here on earth to take care of people and animals; that it's her mission in life. She has taken good care of my older sisters and me for many years.

Linda Snow for answering my call for help so often in fighting my computer. Thank you is not enough.

BOOKS WRITTEN BY SIOUX DALLAS

First Experience

Sharon

Desperate Wish

L i i s a

Death in Three Quarter Time

The Perfect Spouse

Montana Madness

Dangerous Hilarity

Amish Dilemma

And coming soon:

A Detective's Heart

Psalm 53 The fool says in his own heart "There is no GOD."

Proverbs 3:5-6 Trust in the LORD with all your heart and lean not on your own understanding in all ways acknowledge HIM and HE will make your path straight.

The following is an Amish school verse
that school children learn:

I must be a Christian child
Gentle, patient, meek and mild
Must be honest, simple, true
In my words and actions too.
Must remember God can view
All I think and all I do.

Be kinder than necessary for everyone you meet is fighting some kind of battle. Live simply, love generously, care deeply, speak kindly, and leave the rest to God.

****
Amish language taken from the Pennsylvania Dutch dictionary
Bible verses from the New International Version

ACKNOWLEDGEMENTS

My heartfelt thanks to the Yoders at their restaurant in Sarasota, Florida.

I am grateful that they were so patient and kind to answer my many questions about the Bible verses they use and Amish daily living.

They were awarded first place of restaurants by People's Choice Awards.

Local people eat there often and tourists have the address to find them and enjoy the food.

YODER'S AMISH VILLAGE
3434 Bahia Vista Street
Sarasota, Florida
34239

CHAPTER ONE

Charity Startz sat with bowed head with her heart beating so fast it felt as if it were trying to break out of her body. There had been three hours of sermons and songs starting at eight in the morning and going until eleven. There were no musical instruments; they would be considered worldly. A song leader would sing one line and teach it to the congregation.

Everyone memorized the songs and Bible verses.

Charity sat as they all did on a hard bench with no back. They were careful to keep good posture and straight backs. The women sat on one side and the men sat on the other side. Church services were held every other Sunndawk (Sunday) in the home of a member of the congregation. The benches belonged to the group and were taken by wagon to each haus (house) where the service would be held. Women furnished good tasty food to be shared after the long service. Usually people were served lunch and dinner.

Walls could be moved in the homes to make more room, however, in a few homes the members had to sit in various rooms. The preachers would go from room to room teaching and talking loudly enough to be heard by all.

Kinner (children) were taught to be still and quiet. Mothers brought snacks for the very young ones to keep them quiet. Sometimes small children would toddle from mother in one room to daddy in another room. Bad behavior (disturbing the service) was severely disciplined.

########

Today Charity was sitting on a bench facing the center with her attendants called newehockers. This was not a Sunndawk (Sunday) service but a special Dunnahshdawk (Thursday) service in Novembar (November). Her newehockers were three girls whom she considered best friends; Nadine Lapp, Rosemary Raber and Bonnie Lehman.

Facing Charity on another bench sat Adam Kime with his newehockers Lawrence Startz, Kyle Snader and Gerry Raber. Charity glanced at him under her lowered lashes and thought he looked as if he had bitten into a very sour lemon. She understood why he was not happy but it didn't help her feelings at all.

Charity's father Jacob Startz and Adam's father Joshua Kime had been friends since they were small children. They had promised each other their first born to be married and join the two families. Charity as the oldest daughter and Adam as the oldest son had always known they were promised. They liked each other but it was not a love match. Many Amish felt one should marry first and then learn to love each other.

Although the majority of the parents did not select a mate for their child they did expect to be consulted. Approval must be given and both of the intended couples must be baptized and members of the church. A deacon would announce plans for the wedding in a worship service. This is called being published which is the same as being engaged. The young man does not give a ring. He gives a set of china or a lovely battery clock. Everyone in the congregation prepares for the wedding.

The bride's parents plant a big field of celery which is meant to be a blessing and is a spiritual wish for success. Celery is served to eat as well as placed in vases as flowers during the wedding and the dinner following.

The weddings are held between Ocktobar (October) and Dezembar (December) after the fall harvest and are on either a Deenshdawk (Tuesday) or Dennashdawk (Thursday). Communion is taken in the spring and fall.

The bride's parents prepare for the wedding by making furniture, sewing clothes by hand to be given, baking favorite recipes of the bride and helping the bride to fill her hope chest that her father has made for her. In it she has hand made linens, kitchen items, scrapbooks and other favorites.

The service is usually held in the bride's home as a worship service. Bible passages are read by the minister to emphasize the relationship that must be between husband and wife. (1 Corinthians 7:1-3 *Now it is good for a man not to marry, but since there is so much immorality, each man should have one wife and each woman her own husband. A man will leave his father and mother and be united with his wife and the two shall become one flesh.*)

Ephesians 5:31 There is no divorce in the Amish faith (Corinthians 7: 10-11 *But a wife must not separate from her husband. If she does, she must remain unmarried or else be reconciled to her husband. And a husband must not divorce his wife.*) They literally mean "till death do us part".

* * * * *

Bishop Eash called the couple to stand before him after a two and half hour service. Rev. Chupp stepped up and read scriptures; then admonished them as to their duties to each other. They had counseling previously.

The Bishop asked solemnly, "Can you both confess and believe that Gott (God) has ordained marriage to be a union between one man and one woman? Do you also have the confidence you are approaching marriage in accordance with the way you have been taught?"

"Ja," both Charity and Adam responded.

Turning to Adam he continued, "Do you have confidence brother that Gott has provided this, our sister, as a marriage partner for you?"

"Ja," Adam answered nervously.

He asked the same of Charity and she said "Ja" so low she was asked to repeat it.

"Charity, do you vow to be loyal and care for your husband during adversity, affliction, sickness and weakness and to remain together until death?"

With a trembling voice Charity swallowed and bravely said, "Ja."

She bit her lip to keep the tears from falling. She had worked hard to make her light blue dress, white apron and white prayer kapp (cap). She had pricked her fingers many times with the needle. This clothing would be kept to be worn on special occasions, Sunday service or to be buried in. She was hurt that Adam had not looked at her and it was their wedding day.

"Adam, do you vow to be loyal and care for your wife during adversity, affliction, sickness and weakness and remain together until death?"

Adam gulped and said, "Ja."

"And do you both promise together that you will live with each other with love, forbearance and patience and not part from each other until Gott separates you in death?"

They answered "Ja" together.

"Let us rise and pray for those about to be married."

The Bishop then took Charity's right hand and placed it in Adam's left hand. He then placed one of his hands under the joined hands and his other hand on top. He prayed a blessing and asked for the mercy of God for them.

He then said, "Go forth in the Lord's name. You are now man and wife."

There was no kiss, no special acknowledgement and no rings. Adam went to help the men set up the benches for tables to be used for the dinner and Charity went to help the women in the preparation of food and serving it.

The newly married couple sat at a table, called an 'eck', in a corner with their attendants beside them. The meal itself is a feast. The women have lovingly prepared several main dishes in addition to vegetables, fruits and desserts. Six or seven wedding cakes are set aside to be eaten later in the day. Silent prayers are said before each meal and after. The Bishop cleared his throat to alert everyone that he had finished praying silently.

The men, and important people present, are served first, then the women and children. It takes several seatings to serve two hundred or more guests.

Often there will be more than one wedding in a day. Some people travel from one wedding to another and take food with them to share.

Women in the community have helped obtain napkins with the name of the couple and the date on each one. There may be homemade candy placed in small net bags for favors. The main dish, which the women of the church provide, may be hingleflesh (roast chicken) traumata mush (mashed potatoes) gravy, a variety of meats, vegetables, salads and desserts. Water, coffee, cider or lemonade will be served for beverages.

In the afternoon the young people have a singing while the adults visit.

Later there is a dinner and the cakes are served. For the seating of the young people, on the bride's side are the newly married and the published couples.

On the groom's side are the dating couples. Hymn singing follows the dinner.

* * * * *

Charity sat silently beside Adam in his buggy. They were spending their first night together in the bride's home. The following morning Charity got up at five thirty to help her mother with breakfast. Adam went out to help Charity's father feed the animals and clean the sheiyah (barn). The couple then busy themselves cleaning up after the ceremony. Benches must be taken to a place where they are stored until they will be taken to the next haus (house) for a Sunndawk (Sunday) service.

Adam was a willing worker helping Jacob Startz set the milking machines on the kees (cows) and feeding the sixty dairy kees. The milch (milk) was strained and poured into large metal containers and placed on a sled for a gaul (horse) to pull it to the edge of the bavvrkai (farm) property for a truck to pick up the milk and give Jacob a receipt for it. The large containers had markings on them to show who owned those particular containers so the correct people would be paid. Too, the markings helped to keep records of desirable and undesirable milk.

The following weekend Adam hitched his horse to the buggy to take Charity visiting nearby relatives and close friends. This is a honeymoon.

Each house they visited had a gift for them. The gifts could be a handmade item, a plow, a young cow, homemade furniture, or seeds for spring planting. In January they went to live with the groom's parents.

Christmas came with a deep snow which prevented people from visiting or going out. The Amish do not have decorated trees or do any celebrating as the town people do. Some do exchange gifts. The women do make Rinderrouladen, or bake Speingerle cookies, Sugar cookies, Sugar Cream Pie and many other tasty items. Christmas was a time for special worship services, remembering the birth of Christ and reading the story in Luke.

Charity and Adam were busy working and making items for their own home.

Januar (January) and Februar (February) passed slowly because there were so many animals to feed even in the cold and snow. There was lots of outside work to be done and plenty indoors. Women did get together as often as possible for quilting sessions and to make clothes for an expected baby.

Marz (March) came roaring in like a lion which meant they would have an early spring. (The old saying was "In like a lion, out like a lamb")

Jacob Startz and Joshua Kime announced in a worship service that they would be building a house and a barn for Charity and Adam. The Amish all pitch in to help each other and do not consider it an imposition. It is fun.

At six in the morning about six dozen men and boys came to help.

Gauls were turned into a pasture with water so they could rest and graze.

Buggies were lined up as if they were posing for a picture. They were building on land between the two farms to join the two families.

Joshua laughing said he was going to build lots of bedrooms for many kinskinner (grandchildren) he was expecting. Charity blushed but said nothing because she knew she was expecting a boppli (baby) either the last of Septembar (September) or the first of Oktobar (October). She was so happy to be a mother but her heart would have been lighter if Adam had exhibited any signs of being happy to be a father.

Jacob and Joshua had given Adam two Percherons for farm work. His uncle, Noah Kime, had given him a buggy gaul which could also be ridden under saddle. Adam loved that gaul and named her Bonnie Kate.

Moving into their new home was a time for rejoicing and much happiness.

Charity was thrilled to be on their own at last. Adam showed little interest except to thank the people for their help. As they moved into the house on March 20th, Charity had her nineteenth birthday. There was no special gift from her husband. Friends came by with canned foods, flower rootings and handmade items. Her mother had made her three new aprons and two dish towels for the kitchen. Her best aldi (girlfriend), Nadine, gave her a tiny kitten which she named Snowflake because it was all white, fluffy and cuddly. The Zook twins, Christine and Ruth Ann brought a basket of candy they had made and two loaves of Friendship bread.

Adam started plowing and planting his fields while Charity put in a big vegetable garden, an herb garden and lots of flowers. She brought all the bedding out to beat it and hang it in the fresh air for awhile. She took all the curtains down to stretch them on the curtain stretcher and hang them clean and fresh smelling. Two of her friends came to help her wash windows and clean the entire house. It was a Freidawk (Friday) and she and Adam would host the worship service on Sunndawk.

On Samshdawk (Saturday) men brought in the benches and more women came to help Charity prepare the house. She knew everyone would bring food to share but she had been baking and planning food for several days.

This was exciting for Charity because it was the first time she and Adam had entertained. Inside and out everything must be clean.

Charity was so pleased that a huge crowd came to their house. She felt they were accepting Adam and her as a mature couple. She was astonished at the amount of food brought. Her mother whispered that everyone knew she was expecting her first baby and knew how tired she would get. They furnished enough food to leave some for her and Adam.

Adam hired two teenage neighbor boys to help him in the field and to help build whatever was needed for use on the farm. He wanted a separate building for the food stored as feed for the animals and one to park the buggies and work wagons. In the fall they would harvest the crops and put up necessary supplies or sell what had been raised to sell. Charity would can foods and prepare for winter.

Adam and Charity had a stand beside the road in front of their property where they sold vegetables, fruit and honey. Charity included eggs and few baked goods. A few times she sold pots of flowers.

The summer was hot and hard for them. Adam was kind to Charity and was quick to see that she had what was need inside and out, but he was not affectionate. Charity wished with her whole heart that he would once hold her and say "I love you". He was a gentleman and a good husband but didn't think it was necessary to show affection. He felt he was working to provide a good home, plenty of food and that was all that was necessary.

Charity worked hard to be a good wife and a good housekeeper. She was an excellent cook and a very good seamstress. She kept the house neat and tidy, fed some of the animals and took care of the garden. She also helped Adam when he needed her outside.

Charity was pleased to view the many jars of vegetables and fruits she had canned and made ready for winter. These were kept down in a basement.

She would can meats later.

CHAPTER TWO

Late spring and early summer were hotter than usual and Adam worked hard in the field and feeding and caring for the larger gediere (animals). Charity took care of the picks (pigs) and all the fowl.

One Deenshdawk (Tues.) Adam was standing under a tree giving Bonnie Kate a bath. Kyle Snader, Matthew Startz and Gerry Raber were visiting.

"Adam, she sure is a schee (pretty) gaul." Gerry stated as he used a scraper to take the suds off Bonnie Kate.

"Danki, (thank you) I think so," Adam answered. "At first I was naerfich (nervous) riding her on the highway, but she handled beautifully."

"Why would you be nervous? You're one of es bescht (the best) with gauls." Matthew assured him.

"Nee. I'm not the best, but I do love to work with them. It would be so nice if I could afford to open a training school and have an income doing something I really like. Maybe I could ---

"Kumme schnell (come quickly)," Charity called excitedly.

"Why is she so excited?" Gerry asked.

"I don't know, but I'd best go see. She is a good frau, and I know I'm lucky to have her.

"Wie geht's (How are you)?" Kyle asked Charity.

"Gut danki, (good thank you) but the picks (pigs) aren't. The hundel (pup) got into the pack (pen) and frightened the picks. They broke out and are running over the field. They'll tear up what has been planted and will eat what has grown." She was in a dummle (hurry) to tell them, talking so fast and excited that they could hardly understand her.

"So the hundel got into the pack and frightened the picks," laughed Matthew. "We'll get them. Don't worry schwesechder (little sister). Your big bruder is here to help."

The young men ran off to get the picks back in the pack with a lot of laughing and missed tackles. The picks were finally back in the pack and the sides reinforced, and the frisky hundel was tied at the side of the house.

"Oh, danki," Charity laughed. "I could never have done it alone. Can you stay for nachtesse (supper)?

"Nee danki. Mamm (mom) expects me home to eat supper with her and daed (dad)." Matthew grinned. "You know how mamm is."

"Ja, I know. Gern gschehn." (You're welcome any time.)

"Ja, I know. Come on fellows. Are you going or staying for nachtesse?"

"I'm going. I have a koppwveh (headache) and I need to go home and lie down." Kyle said holding his hands on both sides of his head.

"Why do you have a headache?"

"I landed hard once on a rock and hit my head when I dived for a pick. Besides I'm so dreckich (dirty) mamm might not even let me in the haus (house) Kyle laughed.

"You are no dirtier than my husband," Charity laughed. "But if you must leave, know you're gern gschehn to come again. Give my love to our parents." The boys laughed and ran away.

April came in with the heat beginning to build up. Ostar (Easter) was on the next Sunndawk but the Amish do not celebrate as the Englisch do. They tell the story of Christ arising from the grave and what the promise for us is.

Shrove Tuesday is known as Fastnacht (Fat Tuesday)and is the day before Ash Wednesday. The Amish do not celebrate Ash Wednesday. The women make a special dough and place it in a clean cloth in a basket to rise. Later it is cut into squares and fried in deep fat, then sprinkled with confectioner sugar. They are served hot at breakfast where they are cut open and spread with honey or whatever is desired. The Amish know that days of sacrifice are ahead so they think it wise to use up fats and sugars and prepare for a special fast.

Gruna Dunaschdawk (Green Thursday) is the day before Kaofreidawk (good Friday). On Freidawk the families have a special worship service where they are told the story of Christ's torture and entombment. At this service the congregation says the Lord's Prayer (or model prayer) together.

Veter unser im Himmel. Geheiligt werde dein name. Dein Reich komme, dein wille geschehe wie im Himmel so auf Erden. Unser tagliches brot gib uns heute und vergib uns unsure schuld wie auch wir verge Ben unseren schuldigern. Und fuhre uns nicht in versuchung, sondern erlose un von dem bosen. Denn Dein ist das Reich, und die kraft und die Herrlichkeit in ewigkeit. Amen

All through the week the children, while gathering eggs, will hide some for themselves. The ones today are allowed to color their eggs, but not to hide them and hunt. They enjoy looking at each others eggs.

On Sunndawk there is a long service and special food for a thankful day.

They eat well to break the fast. Moondawk (Monday) is set aside to visit and rest. Some of the young men go fishing with friends.

Mai (May) and Juni (June) was more work and little time for leisure. Adam proudly viewed the results of his labor and Charity was pleased with the sewing and cleaning she had done. They could not express their pride and pleasure though because it would be worldly and wrong.

Juli (July) rolled in hot, dry and miserable. Everyone worked to keep water on their crops and gardens or they would dry up and be lost. The entire property was lovely to see. Adam had planted trees and had kept some of the fruit tress that were already on the property.

They had a stream running along the back of their property and a place not far away that held fish. Adam's friends joined him occasionally for fishing and a picnic.

Charity decided to invite some close friends to fish and picnic on their property. One sweltering Mittrodawk, (Wed.) four girls joined her walking to the water. Christine Zook, Rosemary Raber, Bonnie Lehman and Nadine Lapp with Charity made up a group of five. They happily walked along talking of people they knew, of couples planning weddings, new babies expected and daily living on their farms. They carefully went around the bee hives that Adam kept.

Christine giggled, "Charity, do you wish for a buwe (boy) or a maedel (girl)?"

"Adam and I have discussed it and we've decided that we don't care as long as the boppli is healthy. We don't want to stop with just one kinner."

Reaching the water, they paused to admire the clear reflection of the water glimmering like a jewel as it reflected the azure sky and willow trees along the bank.

"Oh," Rosemary giggled, "I don't know about the rest of you but we're only girls here and I'm going to take off my shoes and socks and wade in the shallow end." Rosemary was published and planning on being married in Oktobar. She knew that once she was married she must act like a grown woman. She intended to enjoy the few months left.

"Rosemary!" Nadine as the oldest scolded, "You would have to pull up your dress and show your legs." As a teacher in an Amish school, she felt she should set a good example.

"Poo with that. I'm going to join her," Bonnie laughed. "Come on. Don't be a snickelpuss (spoil sport)." As the youngest she was the most daring.

Nadine sat on the bank. "This is just too beautiful to disturb the water. I love looking at it and feeling the peace it brings."

Christine was timid by nature, but was easily led to join them in the cool water on such a hot day. She hesitated on the bank.

Charity hurriedly removed her shoes and socks and, pulling her dress to her knees, waded into the water. "Oooh, it feels so good. Come on all of you."

She laughed and kicked one foot out to spray the water toward Nadine on the bank. Soon all five girls were in the water, giggling and threatening to get each other wet.

They were enjoying the cool water on such a hot day that they didn't hear Amos Snader and Moses Yoder walk to the water's edge. The girls jumped in shock and guilt when Moses, in his deep voice, yelled out.

"Have you forgotten who you are and where you are? You should be ashamed to be in public showing your limbs. Get out of there right now and make yourselves decent. Your parents will be so ashamed when they hear of this."

The girls hurriedly came out of the water, dropped their dress to the ankles and put on socks and shoes. None of them looked in the face of the men.

Charity was boiling, but was too polite to say anything to the men. Amish women were taught to not speak up and to allow the men to make decisions.

This couldn't keep her from thinking. **This is my property and you are trespassing. Go away and leave us alone**. She was a little angry that she dare not voice her feelings. The men left shaking their heads.

After the men were out of the range of the girls' voices, Rosemary stamped her small foot. "How dare they! Charity this is YOUR property and they had no business telling us what to do."

"Well," Nadine huffed, "who is going to tell them so?"

"Not me," Bonnie said through tight lips. "It makes me so mad that the men, all the men, think they can rule over all us women. One of these days we'll have the right to speak for ourselves and do as we please as long as it is on private property and we're hurting no one. We had no idea a man would be cutting across your property, Charity. And they sneaked up on us."

"We were showing our limbs and knew better than to lift our skirts," Christine timidly stated. They ignored her.

"Do either of you feel like eating now?" Charity asked.

They shook their kobbs (heads), picked up the basket of food and started trudging back to Charity's house.

Charity felt as if she had a stone in her stomach when she saw Adam waiting for them, his fists on his hips and glaring angrily. She resented his attitude but dare not challenge him.

"Charity, get in the house. I think it's time you girls went home," Adam glared at them. The four girls silently hugged Charity and whispered encouragement, then walked quickly off. Charity had all she could take.

"Adam. We did nothing wrong. It was just us five girls and the two men cut across our property. It was none of their business what we were doing. We didn't even get to eat our picnic lunch."

"It was embarrassing to me for the men to come tell me what my wife, my pregnant wife, was doing showing her legs. I need to finish hoeing the weeds and then I'll be in. For nachtesse," he stated firmly.

Charity stomped into the house determined to have a frank talk with her husband. She sure could use a hug now.

Adam came wordlessly into the house just at dusk. He washed his hands, sat at the table and they bowed their heads for silent prayer (Matthew 6:6 *When you pray, go into your room, close the door and pray. Do not keep on babbling like pagans, for they think they will be heard because of their many words. Your Father knows what you need before you ask.*)

They think this means to pray silently and not try to impress others.

Adam stopped and said nothing, but he looked at Charity with a questioning expression.

"This is our supper. The men kept us from eating our lunch and I didn't want the food to go to waste." Adam nodded and began to eat the ham sandwiches placing lettuce, mustard and tomato on it. Deviled eggs, fresh canned pickles, potato cakes and apple pie made up the rest of the meal.

After they had eaten they again bowed in silent prayer. (Deuteronomy 8:10 *When you have eaten and are satisfied, praise the Lord your God.*)

Adam scooted his chair back, placed his right ankle on his left knee and stared at Charity. She couldn't take it.

"Adam, I don't know why you're so mad. We did nothing wrong. In the first place, I was on my own property. We only had the dress lifted to the knees and the lower leg was in the water. They need to keep their naas (nose) out of my business."

Adam's eyebrows went up because Amish women did not show such emotion. He put it down to her pregnancy.

Charity continued, "The way those men acted, you would have thought dunner (thunder) and wedderleech (lightning) was being brought because of us. I'll admit, my hochmut (pride) was hurt, and -- yes, I know I shouldn't feel that way. We were not being nexnutzich (naughty); just cooling off and having a good time together. We were not acting in geheemnis (secret); we were in the open on our own property." She stopped to catch her breath and to take a deep breath to keep from crying.

She started to talk again but Adam held his hand up, palm toward Charity to show he didn't want her to talk.

"I told you it was embarrassing to be told that my wife, my pregnant wife, was showing her limbs in public. After hearing you speak I can see that what you did was not bad enough to create all of that commotion. I'll take care of it. Just let me know what you plan to do in the future."

Charity was trying very hard not to cry but could not stop a few tears rolling down her cheeks.

"Charity, while we're talking I'd like to ask you something. Do you regret marrying me? Is our life disappointing or boring?"

Charity was so disturbed that she jumped up and overturned her chair. "I've been meaning to ask you those same questions."

"Why would you think to ask me about that?"

"You have never hugged me, or kissed me, or said you love me. Are you regretting being married to me?" She was sobbing by now.

Adam jumped up and hurried around the table. He hugged her and she laid her kobb (head) on his shoulder. He finally placed a finger under her chin and gently raised her to face him. He smiled and kissed her. "I do love you. Don't you known I've worked hard to provide for you? I guess I've never seen my parents be affectionate and I just never thought to show you. I feel so blessed to have you. I'm so proud of you and want our marriage to be happy and successful."

Needless to say, bedtime, that night, was all Charity could want it to be.

Adam was trying very hard to be a good, thoughtful husband.

Their gut nacht (good night) was said very lovingly to each other.

CHAPTER THREE

The next morning Charity happily got up at five thirty and went to the kitchen to get breakfast. Adam was out in the barn feeding and caring for the animals. He came in and ate a big breakfast because they had always been taught that breakfast was the most important meal of the day; it was breaking the fast. He had oatmeal, three over easy eggs, fried potatoes, four biscuits with butter and blackberry jam and two glasses of milk.

He sauntered around the table to Charity's back where she was preparing to wash dishes. He put his arms around her and hugged her close. She lay her head back against him and then slowly turned to face him. He smiled and kissed her soundly, then grabbed his hat from a peg on the kitchen wall and almost ran out of the house to start work for the day.

Charity smiled to herself and began to dance around holding her arms out like a small child might. She suddenly realized that she was doing something worldly and stopped, asking God to forgive her. She wanted to do something special for Adam and began to gather materials for making two banana pies with thick meringue just as he loved them. She was singing to herself and busily rolling out dough so that she didn't hear someone come in the kitchen door.

A deep voice said, "Guder mariye, dochder (Good morning, daughter)."

She whirled around so fast she shook flour powder over the table and floor.

"Ah, mi daed, (oh, my dad) I didn't hear you come in."

"Wie geht's?"

"I'm fine, daed, how are you?"

"Gut, gut, although I'm little nunnery (sad)"

"Why daed?"

"Was is letz do (What is wrong here)? Mannsleit (men) are telling stories on you. They even went to the Bishop and asked to shun you."

"Der Herr bilf mir" (The Lord help me) she spoke loudly. I am trying not to be falsch (resentful) but ---"

Adam ran in. "Guder mariye daed Jacob (Good morning dad Jacob). I saw you come in, but had to finish a job."

Charity turned to him and threw her arms around his neck sobbing. She finally was able to tell him what her father had come to talk about. Adam got red in the face.

"Charity is my frau and I lieb (love) her. I resent the nixnootzich (good for nothing) who spreads this manure. My wife was not nockich (naked); she was on her own property, not out in public and only had her feet and calf of her leg in the water. These men are schrooching (twisting) their story and it is shendlich (disgraceful) that they are allowed to tell greislich ligner (horrible lies)."

Adam became even angrier when he heard the men wanted the Bishop to shun Charity. "They are all ob im kopp (off in the head) and need a gut bletching (good whipping)."

By now Jacob was trying hard not to laugh out loud. "Ball wollt's berser geb (soon it will be better). It sounds as if they missverschtch (misunderstood) and blabber maul (talked too much). It is fremt (strange) they didn't come to me before they prattled to the Bishop. I'll talk to him and explain what really happened and he will understand. I'm going to suggest that he bring the men before the congregation and caution them about spreading untrue talk."

"Danki daed Jacob." Adam smiled relieved.

"Gern gschehn (you are welcome)." It is wunderbaar (wonderful) to see a young couple doing so well and taking care of each other. Dochder, your mamm will be relieved to know the truth."

Charity was almost skipping she was so happy and relieved. "Sitz (sit) both of you and I'll give you a piece of pie and a cup of coffee."

"This is so appeditlich (delicious), and I've enjoyed our talk, but I must go." Jacob pushed his chair back. "By the way I hope you're planning on joining your mamm and me tomorrow for the July 4th celebration.

"Ja," Adam answered. "We will be there and I will have some of my wooden animals for sale and Charity has potted plants for sale. We'll see you for sure."

"Gut. Da Herr sei mit du (Good, the Lord is with you). Gott segeneich (God bless you) Wiederschen (Goodbye)." Jacob took his hat off the peg in the kitchen and left.

Charity laughed out loud and leaped at Adam to hug him. He returned the hug with both arms and laying his cheek against hers.

The following morning, Juli 4th, Charity and Adam were up early. He fed the animals, gathered the eggs and completed outside work She was fixing a hearty breakfast and packing food for their midday meal and later.

She packed plenty for them and enough to share.

Driving into town was a headache. Cars, buggies and people walking everywhere. Finally Adam found a section where the buggies were being parked with a fenced-in area for the horses to rest and exercise. He found a good spot for their place to sell their items that was not far from the food booths and arts and crafts booths.

Adam unloaded twelve wooden animals he had made as well as four bird houses and two dog houses. He carefully lifted twenty-four clay pots of flowers, ten pint jars of honey, and four faceless dolls. Leaving Charity to set the booth up he drove the horse to the designated area and unhitched him.

Walking back to Charity he passed a booth of cakes, cookies, pies and breads run by Tobias and Meredith Retstatt who had married early in the spring before planting time. Meredith was plump and jolly and showing signs that a boppli would be with them soon.

Adam called a pleasant greeting to the young couple and appreciatively sniffed the air. "Guder mariye," he called to them. "Webishtew? (How are you?)"

"Wunderbaar," they answered. "Wie geht's?"

"Gut. Gut, danki. To smell your appeditlich kichlin (delicious cookies) makes my mouth water. I'll get some later." He hurried back to Charity.

Charity was thrilled that she had already sold two of his animals, one of her dolls and several flowers and all the honey. Surprisingly they sold out fast to the Englisch. These were tourists buying the dolls to take home and display.

To hers and Adam's delight, they sold out quickly.

Adam asked Charity if she felt like walking to the other booths and looking. She laughing said, "Can you keep up with me?" They had not gone far until they became aware of a disturbance. Adam was appalled to discover an unpleasant confrontation between Amish young men and town young men. As he drew near he discovered Kyle Snader, Gerry Raber, Connie Lehman and Cordero Slabough were involved. He recognized the faces of two of the townies, but didn't know their names. He was upset to see several young men from town and several Englisch adults standing around not trying to stop the angry jeering and name calling. His heart gave a quick jump because he knew Kyle had a bad temper and could control it only so long in spite of their Amish teaching.

"Stay back here where you won't get hurt," he cautioned Charity. "I'm going to try to reason with them.

"Oh, Adam, should you? I'm afraid you might get hurt."

"I need to help my friends," he smiled walking off. As he drew near he heard two of the town boys calling out insults and shoving the Amish boys.

"Where'd ya get that funny haircut? It looks like a bowl was placed on your head and cut around it."

"Yeah. Why do you wear such funny clothes? They look uncomfortable."

Adam stepped in front of Kyle still smiling. "Good morning, gentlemen. Is there something I can do for you?"

"Hey, look. Here's another funny looking one and he's trying to be like all the rest of us." One of the boys shoved Adam. He just stood firm and didn't answer.

Rachael Snader, Rosemary Raber and Charity had slipped closer. Charity had heard all she could take. She hurried to Adam's side with a determined gleam in her eyes.

"Shame on you. You're picking on men who are taught to be peaceful and not be abusive to anyone. They are not bothering you. Why are you being so cruel? What have any of us ever done to you?"

Adam sucked in a startled and angry breath. "Charity, this concerns the men. Please go back and wait for me."

"Hoo eee. Would you listen to this? Your women have more guts and courage than you men do. Are you going to let them stand and fight for you, too?"

Adam placed a firm arm around Charity and backed off with her. He glared at her and left her standing beside the other girls. All three girls immediately pushed forward. Rachael and Rosemary to stand by their brothers and Charity by her husband.

Luckily for them Sheriff Micah Fleming had been summoned and he arrived just as the girls stepped forward. Two deputies followed.

"What's going on here?" his deep voice boomed out. "I have a county to take care of and you young men are not making my job any easier." He glared at the town boys. "I know all of you and I know your parents would be upset with your actions."

"Not mine," Ashley Wilkins sneered. "My father thinks they should be run out of the country."

"Why?" the sheriff asked. "What have they done to you?"

"Nothing to us, but they won't pay taxes, or vote or take responsibility for the rules and regulations of our country." Douglas Winthrop sneered. "My dad says so and he knows what he's talking about."

"You've been given some terribly wrong information. They DO pay taxes and they uphold law and order. They don't draw welfare or accept food stamps; they take care of their own. Therefore, they are not a liability to our country. In fact they work hard, improve the land and teach their children to be respectful, law abiding citizens. We need more like them." Fleming said.

"Yeah, yeah, yeah. Just wait. With your attitude, you'll be voted out of office next fall." Darren Kennedy boasted.

"I'm not worrying about the election," he said. "If I do my job and serve all citizens and protect all citizens, then my conscience is clear. Go on now and don't cause any more trouble or I'll have to arrest you."

That evening the Amish banded together to sit on quilts to watch the fireworks and enjoy the music from a band and a choir.

There was a beautiful display of fireworks ending with a red rose in the sky and the American flag. They all shared the food they'd brought. When everyone stood to place their hands over their hearts and sing the National Anthem, the Amish stood respectfully and proudly participated. This ended the day's activities.

CHAPTER FOUR

Two days after the fourth, Charity was still upset that the town people were so cruel to them for no reason except the Amish were different. Her parents had taught her to be kind and forgiving to everyone even those outside their faith.

Charity was weeding her vegetable and herb gardens while Adam was, as usual, working in the field. She was astonished to see a bright red, expensive car driven up their driveway and parking near her. She stood still and watched a woman step out.

The woman was dressed in a light blue silk sleeveless shirt with darker blue shorts. She wore big gold hoop earrings and several dangling bracelets.

There was even a gold bracelet around her left ankle. She walked in high-heeled sandals to Charity with a big smile on her face as if she thought Charity should be impressed with her.

Charity waited for the woman to speak.

"Good afternoon. I hope you're Mrs. Kime. Sheriff Fleming told me your name and where to find you."

Charity nodded but still said nothing. She rubbed one bare foot against the other and took a slow step toward the woman.

The woman stepped closer with her hand held out. "My name is Lisa Kennedy. That naughty boy, Darren Kennedy is my son. I must apologize for his behavior in the park. He was certainly not raised to act in that manner. His father, Dr. Willfred Kennedy, is a dentist in town and he is very ashamed at the behavior of our son. Sheriff told the parents of all the boys about the misfortune and I wanted to ask your forgiveness."

Charity took a deep breath not knowing what to say. She had never in her life been face to face with an outsider like this.

"Ma'am----"

"No. Call me Lisa."

Charity smiled. "My name is Charity."

"Charity! What a beautiful name. Do you live up to the name? Oh, how rude of me. I meant nothing by it; I was just trying to be friendly, and, to tell the truth, I'm a little nervous about coming here, but my husband insisted, and you know how husbands can be." She gave a nervous giggle.

Charity smiled weakly and said, "Mrs. Kennedy, it is our religion and how we're raised to not show anger, not quarrel with anyone and not be ugly to anyone for any reason. We are to be passive, forgiving, and kind. I was upset because, even if your son had hit one of our men, they would not have been allowed to hit back."

"That is wonderful. Do you really live by that?"

"Oh, ja. If we did not the church would punish us for it."

"I take it yah means yes. How would the church punish you and why would they make it their business?"

"The community, all the families, make up the church. We have a set of rules and regulations that we must follow. If we do not, it brings shame to everyone. We would be punished by being meidung, that means shunned."

"What does it mean to be shunned?"

"You are ignored by everyone. Family cannot eat with you or have anything to do with you. If you're married the husband, or wife, cannot have any contact with you until the shunning is over. It's almost as if you died or moved away."

"That's awful. I am a member of the big church you saw on the corner. We would be careful not to do anything that we would be ashamed of. If we did do something wrong, the church members might talk to us and pray with us, but they would never act as if we did not exist."

There was a short silence as the woman thought and Charity tried to assimilate the rules of the woman's church. While there was silence, Adam ran to them. He placed an arm around Charity and looked at the woman.

"Hi. I assume you're Mr. Kime. I'm Lisa Kennedy. I was just telling your wife that Darren Kennedy, my son, was one of the bad boys who gave you and your friends a hard time at the park. My husband and I are so sorry about it and hope you'll be understanding."

Adam was pleasant but not friendly. "We do not hold grudges and we cannot fight or return bad behavior if it comes to us."

"Your wife, Charity," she said with a big grin to them, "just explained all of that to me. Well, I know you're busy. I must be going. Oh, could I visit your church some time?"

"We do not have a special building. We meet in each other's homes. You would be welcomed, but I don't believe you would be comfortable. Our services are three to four hours long with a meal following."

"Wow! That long." She laughed. "I get restless when ours lasts an hour."

She told them goodbye and left. Charity had felt uncomfortable being in the company of a grown woman showing her legs, arms and neck in that manner. And those shoes!

Adam looked at Charity with raised eyebrows. She told him of the entire conversation.

"I'm sorry you had to face that. The poor woman has no shame to come out in public and in front of men dressed like that. We will pray for her and her family."

Adam trudged back to the field while Charity continued her work.

The next Saturday Adam came running into the house breathless and looking distressed. "Cordero Slabough just came to tell me bad, very bad news." He stopped to get his breath. "Kyle, Gerry, Buckley and Lawrence took some produce into town to sell at the market. Those Englisch boys saw them and started in on them again. They kept pushing Kyle until he fell backward. He got up angry. When the Sheriff got there the Kennedy boy had to be taken to the hospital and the other boys were cut and bruised. Kyle had taken a bad beating, as had the Amish boys, trying to stop the fight, got hurt as well. They are all now under arrest, Amish and town boys."

"Lawrence, my bruder?!"

"Ja."

"Oh, daed will skin him. Mercy they will all be meidung."

"Maybe, maybe not. When the Bishop hears about it, he'll make the decision. I'm sure he'll understand the situation," Adam comforted.

"I need to pray a lot about this," Charity moaned.

"We'll both pray, and I know the families and the church will be praying."

"Adam, please go with me to my parents and find out what is happening to my bruder."

"Give me a few minutes to put my tools away and see to the animals, and I'll be happy to go with you. Why don't you take some of the baking you've been doing to share while I get the buggy ready."

Adam ran out to tend to his business while Charity wrapped two loaves of Friendship bread and some special cookies she had baked.

At the Startz home Charity was astonished to see her daed out working in the fields and her mamm hanging a wash. She jumped down from the buggy in such a hurry that it worried Adam.

"Charity, don't do anything that will hurt the boppli."

She ran to hug her mother and ask why she was doing her usual work. By the time they got settled in the house, Jacob came in. Her grandparents came out of the dawdi haus (grandparents house) to join them. Charity was so worried she was gulping to keep from crying.

Grossdawdi Mishler (Grandfather) suggested they pray before they talked.

He held the Biewel (Bible) while he prayed.

Charity could hardly wait for the prayer to be over. "But why were Kyle and Lawrence arrested for just defending themselves?"

Jacob looked sternly at her and quoted: *Jesus said, you have heard an eye for an eye and tooth for tooth, but I tell you do not resist an evil person. If someone strikes you on the right cheek, turn to him the other also.* (Matthew 5:38-39) He then quoted: *For if you forgive men when they sin against you, your Heavenly Father will also forgive you. But if you do not forgive men their sins, your Father will not forgive your sins.* (Matthew 6:14-15)

"That's all true and good," Charity blurted, "but they did fight to defend themselves. Won't the Sheriff understand that?"

"Ja," Jacob answered, "but he has a job to do and he had to arrest all that were involved until it can be settled in court."

"In court! You mean there'll be a trial? That is not something we approve of and will not take part in." Charity was breathless with concern.

"Dochder, calm down. Sometimes things happen that we cannot control and we have to cooperate with the Englisch. We'll be forced to appear in court and maybe even pay a lawyer."

Grossdawdi quoted: *But those who hope in the Lord will renew their strength. They will soar on wings like eagles; they will run and not grow weary; they will walk and not be faint.* (Isaiah 40:31)

Jenna Mae (Charity's mother) timidly quoted: *We also rejoice in our sufferings because we know that suffering produces perseverance, character and hope. And hope does not disappoint us because God has poured out His divine love into our hearts by the Holy Spirit whom He has given us.* (Romans 5:3)

Jacob cleared his throat, patted his wife on the back and said: *A foolish son brings grief to his father and bitterness to the one who bore him.* (Proverbs 17: 25)

Charity was so upset that she jumped up and started pacing. "I don't know how all of you can sit there and calmly quote Biewel verses when your own flesh and blood is in trouble. It is my understanding that Lawrence was not part of the fight, but was attempting to stop the fight and hold Kyle off."

Adam got up to place an arm around her waist and bring her back to her seat. "Calm down, little mother. We've only just heard the news and we don't know all that has happened. I have faith that the Sheriff will act in a responsible manner and do what is right for all concerned."

"For all concerned." She spat out the words, "The Englisch have no right to be given consideration because they are the ones who always make fun of our Amish clothing, speech and the way we live." She jumped up again.

"Ja," Jacob agreed nodding his head, "but that doesn't excuse us if we lose our temper and cause more hard feelings or trouble for others."

Charity stamped her foot. "Why must we always be the ones who back down and be the peacemaker?"

Her mother calmly walked to Charity. "Because we believe in the Word of our Lord and do everything we possibly can to live by it."

Jacob looked sadly at Charity. "Your temper is not acceptable for a good Amish woman."

"Daed, I'm sorry, but I'm so worried and afraid."

Adam cleared his throat and stated: *Cast your cares on the Lord and He will sustain you. He will never let the righteous fall, but You, oh God, will bring down the wicked.* (Psalm 55: 22-23)

"Now you're doing it," Charity was almost sobbing. "We're sitting around doing a lot of talking and quoting Biewel verses when we should be out doing something about the unfairness to our community."

"What would you suggest we do, dochder?" Jacob asked calmly.

"Find those Englisch boys and their parents and have a good talking to them."

Grossmudder (grandmother) spoke which was unusual for her. *Do not repay evil for evil. Do not take revenge. It is mine to avenge; I will repay says the Lord.* (Romans 12:17-19)

Charity sat by her mother and looked tight-lipped, but said nothing more.

They talked awhile longer and prayed more. Jacob and Adam said that they would go to court when the young men were brought before a judge.

It is true, they did not believe in taking anyone to court or being involved in a trial. In rare cases the Bishop might give someone permission to appear in court as a witness. However, if arrested, there is no getting around appearing in court as charged.

Jacob led his family in prayer again. Jenna Mae offered to feed everyone, but Adam wanted to get home. He was proud of Charity, but was a little uneasy that she spoke out, and to men, as Amish women do not do.

CHAPTER FIVE

Micah Fleming's wife, Anita, offered to drive her car and take them to court on the day assigned. Jacob, Amos Snader, Isaac Slabough and Moses Yoder gratefully accepted her offer and dressed in their best to be in town.

Each wore the traditional black trousers, white shirt and black hat. They didn't know what to do about money until the judge would tell them if there was to be a fine.

The men sat stoically on a bench behind the Amish young men. Lawrence was ashamed to look at his father and knew what he would have to face at home when, and if, he got out of here. Kyle was so battered that Jacob thought it would be impossible to charge him with an assault. The others sat with heads down and showing fear of the unknown. They knew they had been taught not to lift a hand in anger or say anything in an angry manner.

The young men from town were brought in and seated on another bench on the same side of the room as the Amish. Darren Kennedy smirked as he passed the Amish. Conrad Bolling, Denver Whitmore, Ashley Wilkins, Douglas Winthrop, Marshall Porter, Alan Barkley, Earl Staunton, Abner Washington and Liam McDonald walked in looking smug and satisfied with themselves. After all, they lived in the town and those Amish were not wanted and had no business being in town, they thought.

The bailiff called the court to order and announced that Judge Melinda Pierson would be presiding. The Amish men look startled that a woman was on the bench. They began to feel doubtful about the outcome. Surely a town woman would favor the town boys.

Judge Pierson cracked the gavel and announced that she would not stand for any disrespect toward the court or toward anyone in the court. She reminded them that this was not a trial but a meeting to decide if there would be a court case and what would be expected. She asked the bailiff, Bill White to bring Sheriff Micah Fleming to the stand.

It was difficult to tell from the sheriff's face how he felt. He gave his full name and title. The judge asked him to proceed.

"Last Saturday, July 23rd, I was working on my report to the town council when Pete Mulanaugh came rushing into my office. Pete owns the Tasty Bite Restaurant across the street from the court house. He said there was a big fight going on and he had observed young men from town harassing and taunting some Amish boys. He didn't see how the fight started but was sure the Amish had not started it because everyone knows they are peaceful. I got my hat and ran out calling for Deputy John Lynn and Deputy Roy Braun to follow. When I ran the two blocks and got where I could see, I saw one young man haul off and kick the stuffing out of a young man on the ground. He was Amish and badly hurt. I ran up and ordered them to stop. A couple of the boys from town ran and I didn't get them. My deputies came with two vehicles and I arrested everyone until I could make sense out of the disgraceful brawl. The Amish young men have been respectful and mannerly. The town young men have been arrogant, loud, quarrelsome and hard to contend with."

The judge thanked the sheriff and dismissed him. He left the witness stand and sat in the court room. The judge looked sternly at all the boys on the front benches. She then asked the bailiff to call Pete Mulanaugh to come to the witness chair.

Pete got up from the back of the court room and came forward. He, too, was sworn in and settled nervously to answer questions.

He knew if he angered the town parents, his business would suffer, but he also knew that God had commanded to not give false testimony.

The judge smiled and said, "Mr. Mulanaugh, we apologize for taking you away from your business, however, I need for you to tell us how you first observed this --- this-- disgraceful occurrence."

"Yes, your honor, I'll be happy to tell you what I can. I own the Tasty Bite Restaurant across the street from the courthouse. I'm thankful to have such good business from both the people in town and the Amish. I even have two Amish girls as waitresses." He turned to smile at the judge, but faced front and continued talking much too rapidly in his nervousness.

"Mr. Mulanaugh, please talk so that the Court Reporter can take your statement."

He gulped. "Yes, your honor. Well, I was at the front counter taking money from a customer that was just leaving. A man and a woman. The woman had started out the door but turned around to say that there was a big fight going on about a block near the Feed and Tack Store. The man rushed to join her and I was right behind them. I saw there was indeed a fight. This is unusual, so I called to one of the waitresses to tell her that I would be back shortly. I ran toward the fight and, as I got closer, I could see there were a lot of young men and some of them were Amish. Just then one of the Amish men was knocked down and three of the town men proceeded to kick him. I yelled, but they paid no attention to me. Apparently someone had already called the Sheriff because he ran up just as I got there. He and his deputies started pulling the men apart and he tried to get them to stop and talk to him. Some of the men from town wouldn't stop, so he arrested all of them saying he would take them all in until he got to the bottom of it. Two of the men from town looked as if they had taken some hard licks. I heard some men standing around say the men from town had started it all."

"Thank you, Mr. Mulanaugh, I appreciate your input, but I can't take hearsay talk as facts. I must have the actual people here to tell us what they observed and heard."

"I'm sorry, your honor, but I think the people were tourists, or at least from another town near us."

"Thank you, Mr. Mulanaugh, I appreciate your sharing with us. You may be excused."

Judge Pierson looked at her notes for a minute and then looking up said, "I see the Prosecuting Attorney is present, but I don't see Attorneys for the young men present."

At that moment there was a flurry of activity at the door and a man came running in. He was so tall and thin he looked like Ichabod Crane. His black hair was a little longer than his collar. His black eyes were so prominent that they looked bugged out. His thin lips were drawn tight as he rushed in with coat tail flapping. His gray suit, white shirt and blue tie looked as if he'd slept in his clothes.

"Sorry, your honor. I'm Ezekiel Marshall. I've just this morning been hired by Dr, Willfred Kennedy to represent his son and any of his friends who have need of my services."

"That's fine, Mr. Marshall. I hope you understand we are not having a trial this morning. We're listening to facts to determine if there should be a trial."

"Yes, your honor. I mean, no, your honor. I'm not aware of the entire situation. May I ask for a delay to talk to my client, or clients? If this could be postponed until sometime tomorrow, I would appreciate it."

"Mr. Marshall. I repeat. This is not a trial, however, I appreciate your dilemma. As it is 11 o'clock, I shall adjourn until two o'clock this afternoon. That should give all of us time for lunch and to get our wits together." Judge Pierson tapped her gavel on the pad and stood up.

"All rise," the bailiff quickly called, looking confused.

The Amish fathers looked to Jacob to know what to do. He quickly walked to the gate leading into the area where the young men were seated.

Calling to the bailiff he asked what was going on and if the Amish fathers could talk to the Amish young men.

"I don't see why you can't talk to them. They can't leave to have lunch with you. They'll be fed here."

"Thank you. I just want to talk to my son." He walked to Lawrence and they looked at each other with fear, shame and deep concern.

"Got segen eicg, my buwe (God bless you my boy)." Lawrence hung his head and took deep breaths to keep from crying.

"Daed, how is mamm? I'm so sorry that I brought this on all of you. Kyle was being beaten by three at once and I tried to separate them. I didn't strike any blows and didn't try to fight. I was just trying to separate them and stop the fight."

"Then how did you get that black eye?"

"Someone hit me when I was trying to pull some of them apart."

"Did you see who?"

"Nee daed. There was too much going on and there were twice as many of them as there were of us."

Moses Yoder had been standing by listening. "Didn't anyone else try to stop it?" He was so upset he forgot to speak English.

"A man was coming out of the feed store just as it started," Buckley Yoder remembered.

"Maybe we can find who it was." Moses said with a tremble in his voice.

When they returned from lunch a women came hurrying into the court room. "Oh, I hope I'm not too late."

"Too late for what?" Jacob asked politely.

"My husband and I saw all of this start when we were in the feed store."

"Where is your husband?"

"In the hospital. He tried to stop it and got knocked down. Someone stepped on him and caused bleeding in his chest. We went to the hospital and I just today heard there was to be a hearing. I'd like to help."

The bailiff and deputies, who were keeping an eye on the people, came over and asked everyone to go to their places.

"Sir, my husband and I were in the feed store and saw everything just as it started." She spoke to the bailiff.

"I'll inform the Judge. Please take a seat. All rise. The honorable Judge Melinda Pierson is prepared to continue the hearing."

As she sat at her station the bailiff stepped up and whispered to her. She looked out at the court room, found Mrs. Bledsoe, nodded and whispered to the bailiff.

"The court is now in session. Mrs. Anita Bledsoe, please come forward."

Anita hurried through the gate and stood by the bailiff facing the judge.

Judge Pierson smiled at her. "Mrs. Bledsoe, do you have facts that you would like to share with us concerning this fight?"

"Yes, your honor and I think what I have to say will expedite this hearing."

"Fine. Bailiff, swear her in and show her to the witness stand."

"Place your left hand on the Bible and raise your right hand. Do you swear to tell the truth and nothing but the truth?" he asked.

She hesitated. "Yes, and so help me God I will. I don't approve of that line being left out."

The judge turned to Mrs. Bledsoe. "Please tell us what you observed and how you reacted."

"Yes, your honor. My husband and I were in the Feed and Tack store. I was waiting on my husband to finish a transaction and looked out the window. I saw these young Amish men walking by and minding their own business. Suddenly that one," she pointed to Darren Kennedy, "stepped in front of them with several more behind him. I couldn't hear what was being said, but from the smirk on his face I knew it wasn't good."

"I object," Attorney Marshall jumped up.

"What are you objecting to, Mr. Marshall. To the lady telling the truth?" Judge Pierson asked

"Mrs. Bledsoe said she inside the store and couldn't hear what was being said. She called his expression a smirk, but maybe she saw something that wasn't really there."

The judge drew a deep breath. "Mrs. Bledsoe, would you truly say it was a smirk on this young man's face?"

"Oh, yes. The other young men with him started talking and looking as if they were taunting the Amish young men."

"Your honor! I object."

"This lady has already stated that she could not hear what was being said. How does she know what they were saying?"

"She didn't say she knew. She said it **looked as if** they were taunting."

"Well, what she's saying is making it sound worse than what it was."

"Please have a seat Mr. Marshall. Remember this is only a hearing. Please continue, Mrs. Bledsoe."

"I called to my husband and he and the store owner came to stand beside me. I saw that the Amish men were not showing any signs of anger while the others were looking angry and twisting their mouths to say things. At that moment," she pointed to Darren, "that young man started shoving that young man in the chest." She pointed to Kyle. "Before my husband could get out of the door other young men from town had joined the group and they were shoving the young Amish men around. None of the Amish fought back." She pointed to Darren again. "He took his fist and hit him," pointing to Kyle, "in the chest so hard that he fell backward. Several of the others started kicking him and fighting the Amish. One young Amish man", she pointed to Lawrence, "was begging everyone to stop and was trying to drag the men off the Amish men. All of the town men then started hitting the Amish men and continued until the sheriff came up."

Mr. Marshall jumped up. "Then how did Douglas Winthrop end up in the hospital with a concussion?"

"I can answer that, your honor," Mrs. Bledsoe said.

"Did you see what happened?"

"Yes, your honor."

"Please tell us."

"I don't know any of the names, but I did see some of the town boys so close together trying to fight the Amish that one boy apparently lost his balance and fell backward striking his head on a concrete flower container in front of the feed store. I'm no doctor, but I imagine that's how he got the concussion."

"Then," Judge Pierson said, "are you saying the young men from town struck the first blows and antagonized the Amish men?"

"As far as I could see, they struck the only blows."

A commotion in the middle of the room caused everyone to look that direction. Two men came walking by the Amish fathers and gave them dirty looks.

"Your honor, my name is Quincy Winthrop. May I respond to this lady's testimony?"

"Yes, of course. Mrs. Bledsoe you may be excused, but don't leave yet. Bailiff, bring Mr. Winthrop to the stand and swear him in. And who are you?" she spoke to the second man standing.

"Your honor, I am Dr. Willfred Kennedy, father of Darren Kennedy. I have a say in this." He glared at the Amish men, but did reluctantly sit.

Quincy Winthrop walked with great importance to the witness stand. He placed his hand on the Bible and listened to the bailiff ask him for the truth.

The bailiff again left out 'so help me God'. Winthrop smirked at Mrs. Bledso when he didn't put in the phrase.

"All right Mr. Winthrop, may we hear what you have to say?"

"Oh, yes," he said emphatically. "My son is a Christian and was raised in a Christian home. He has been taught to have compassion on those less fortunate than him," he smirked at the Amish, "and I know for a fact he would never indulge in something as low as a fight."

The judge smiled. "Can we ever be sure what our children will do or say when they are out of our sight or when with others they might be trying to impress their friends?"

"Oh, yes, your honor. I asked him and he told me he didn't fight and that the Amish men were hitting them. I believe my son." He smiled at his son.

Jacob stood up. "Your honor. It's going against our religious training to even be in court. I feel I must say something to clear this up."

"Please do. Bailiff, escort Mr. Winthrop off the stand and swear in Mr.-- May we have your name?"

"Jacob Startz, your honor. My son is Lawrence Startz."

He sat in the witness chair. "Your honor, I mean no disrespect, but we don't approve of swearing and I would like to be excused from that part."

Trying not to smile, Judge Pierson said, "Well, do you affirm that you will tell the truth?"

"Yes, your honor. I have to. If I tell a lie, I will be punished for it."

Not wanting to get into religious discussions with him, the judge asked him to tell what he wanted them to know.

"Your honor, I was not there and did not witness the fight. I can only tell you that our young people are taught to turn the other cheek. If any of them fight, get caught telling lies or spreading hurtful gossip, they will be brought up before the church and shamed. If it is bad enough they will face meinding."

"What is that Mr. Startz?"

"Oh, that is shunning. For about six weeks they would be as if they are dead. Not even family members can eat with them, speak to them or do anything with them. You are not shunned if you have not been baptized and joined the church. All of these Amish boys have been baptized and joined the church. They would be shunned if they lifted their hands in anger against anyone. That is how I know they did not fight. It would bring shame to the entire family, and to the church."

"Thank you, Mr. Startz, I am aware of your beliefs and feel reasonable sure that the Amish young men did not fight."

Mr. Marshall jumped up at the same time Mr. Winthrop and Mr. Kennedy did. All three of them started to argue with her at the same time.

She hit the gavel smartly on the pad. "Gentlemen, and I hope you are, please sit down and keep quiet. I feel I've heard enough to know if there will be a trial. I know for a fact that the Amish will not even defend themselves. As for taking the other young men to court, I leave that up to the Amish whether they will sue or not. They certainly have a case."

Again the three men jumped up to argue.

"Please sit down and be quiet or I'll have the deputies arrest you."

She then turned to the people in the court. "Mr. Startz, and all of your sons and friends. I offer a deep, heartfelt apology for the horrendous behavior of these other young men. It is apparent to me that they lack proper home training and I strongly advise their parents to talk to them about harassing and fighting people just because they are different. I'm going to dismiss all of you, but leave it up to the Amish whether they wish to press charges."

Jacob shook his head. "Your honor, that is against our religion. We must forgive or our Lord cannot forgive us."

"That's all I need to hear." She looked at the town young men. "If I hear even a hint of any of you being involved in anything like this again, you won't have to wait to determine whether you will be sued. I will bring you up on charges." She glared at their fathers. "And I might even include the parents in that. Go in peace."

She hit the pad with her gavel. "Deputies, follow the Amish out first and make sure they leave safely."

Sheriff Fleming stood up to follow them also. There was relief and anger flowing among the crowd leaving the room.

Judge Pierson waited until the bailiff came back in and nodded to him.

"The rest of you may be dismissed. I want all of you to think carefully about the golden rule."

She left her bench and thankfully went back to her office.

CHAPTER SIX

Jenna Mae had waited with Charity while the men were at the court house. Both women were weak with relief when Mrs. Fleming pulled into the driveway and Jacob and Lawrence got out. Jacob tried to pay her, but she refused.

"Danki. Gott segen eich," Jacob told her sincerely.

"Thank you, Jacob, and God bless all of you. I was sure it would turn out the way it did."

She backed up and drove off while Jenna Mae and Charity tried to hug Lawrence at the same time.

Adam hurried in from the field to welcome them and hear about Lawrence's problems.

All of the Startz children were present. Matthew, Alicia, Maeve and Joseph gathered around their brother to hear about all of Lawrence's adventures as Maeve called it.

Charity was so relieved and flustered she could hardly think. "Everyone kumme esh (come eat). Don't baddere (bother) with the shoes."

Charity was so excited and happy that she could hardly talk. "Kumme, sitz and eat yourself full," she told everyone. "I have bohnesuppe (bean soup) and cornbread. There is bread pudding aplenty."

There was the silent prayer before they ate. Jacob was so pleased to have his son home without the trouble he had expected, that he broke tradition and prayed aloud.

Charity had pickled beets, corn on the cob and a cabbage salad. The food was delicious, but it was more so because of the joy and relief.

Two weeks went by with the usual work, Samshdawk visiting and Sunndawk service. The entire community was at peace and all was going well. One Freidawk morning, Kyle thought he would please his father and get up early to do the barn chores. At five he was up and dressed and out to the barn. He greeted the gauls who nickered with pleasure knowing he was going to feed them. The kees lowed hoping they would be fed and milked soon.

Kyle went to the back of the barn and had to light a lantern. He swung it up and then gasped almost dropping it. He caught it knowing if he dropped it there would be a fire. What he saw was unbelievable. A body. A man lying on his face in the hay. It was someone from town because he was not dressed as the Amish do.

Kyle was still standing there not moving when Amos walked in. "Gott in himmel, buwe. (God in Heaven, boy). Are you trying to burn the place down?" He could see Kyle was trembling.

He could not answer his dad; just pointed. Amos hurried over to see what had Kyle so upset. "Was is letz do?" He then saw the body and ran closer to see better. "Who is it?"

"I don't know, daed. He's on his face."

"We must not touch. The sheriff will want to see everything as it is."

Oliver came in, yawning broadly, to help get the kees ready for milking.

Amos took him by a shoulder and would not let him see the body. "Oliver, we must call the sheriff."

"How daed? We don't have a phone."

"Run to our Englisch neighbors, the Morrisons and ask them to call the sheriff for us."

Amish children are taught not to question. Oliver took off in a run and then stopped quickly, his bare feet raising dust.

"What shall I tell them is wrong. Why are you calling him?"

"Just make the call and tell the sheriff it's very important."

Oliver took off as fast as he could run. He was back soon and anxious to know why the sheriff was needed.

"Never mind, buwe, just go in and tell your mamm that we've called the sheriff."

Sarah came hurrying out anxious to see what was going on. Amos met her at the door and whispered to her. She gasped and started to walk closer to the body, but he would not let her.

"We must not get close. There might be something the sheriff could use to determine who killed him."

"Who is it?"

"We don't know yet. He's on his face and we must not touch him."

Sirens were heard and soon Sheriff Fleming rushed in with a deputy car close behind him. He hurried out of the car leaving the door open.

"What is it, Amos? What's the trouble?"

"Kumme, look in the sheiyah."

They walked into the barn where Kyle was still standing as if he were too afraid to move.

Sheriff Fleming looked worried and moved close to the body. "Who is it?"

"I don't know. I would not let anyone touch anything until you got first look."

"Thank you. That's wise. Too many times people destroy clues without meaning to do so."

"Herb," he called to a deputy. "Bring the camera and latex gloves."

The sheriff took pictures of the body and all around it as well as the distance from the door to the body. Pulling on latex gloves he and the deputy carefully rolled the body over to the back.

"Well, I'll be -- Amos come look."

Amos and Kyle moved carefully closer to look at the face of the man.

Kyle gasped. "It's Darren Kennedy. He's the one that has been causing me and others so much trouble. Who killed him and how did he get here?"

"Well now, son. Those are my questions. What do you know about this?"

"N-n-nothing. I didn't even know he was in here."

"A dead person doesn't just walk in and lay himself down."

Amos was more disturbed than ever. "How was he killed?"

"The medical examiner will tell us that. Did either of you hear anything during the night that was unusual?"

"Nee," Amos shook his head. "We didn't know until we came out to do our work and found him."

The sheriff turned to Kyle. "Son, I know you could not kill anyone, but since this boy went out of his way to cause trouble for you his family will probably accuse you and demand action. I know your religion does not encourage having an attorney or going to court, but you'd better be prepared."

The Medical Examiner and his assistant pulled up with a van and a stretcher. Warren Barker had been ME for several years and was well acquainted with the Amish and their beliefs. "Who would do this and put the body in your barn?"

"I don't know, Warren," Amos replied sadly. "I'm hoping you can tell us something that will help."

"Amos, I'll do the very best I can."

The medical report came back that Darren had ingested a powerful poison. His father denied having any around their house and loudly declared that, "Those Amish have a lot of poison around their barns and fields." The ME determined poison had apparently been mixed in a muffin recipe.

Sarah was appalled. "I would never, for any reason, put poison of any kind in my food. He got it somewhere besides here."

Adam was worried for Kyle. He knew how sometimes circumstantial evidence can look bad. He knew people would remember the fight in town and claim that Kyle was angry and either gave the poison to Darren or had someone do it for him. Anyone who knew anything about the Amish knew they would not even defend themselves and they certainly would not commit murder.

Bishop Eash called a special service for the congregation to pray together and give moral support to the Snader family. Benjamin Lapp and Joseph Lehman came to Amos after the service and told him they were with him.

"We'll be ready to help you any way we can," Benjamin explained. "If you need us to go somewhere with you and give support, we're ready."

Joseph placed a hand on Amos' shoulder. "If you do have to hire an attorney and Bishop Eash approves, we'll make sure you have the money."

Amos and Sarah were grateful for such good friends, but they knew that the entire Amish community stood together in any difficult situation.

There was a quiet funeral for Darren. Only relatives and close friends were notified of place and time. Sheriff Fleming hoped the Kennedy family had decided to be low key and not cause trouble for the Amish. He was more at ease now that the funeral was over and there was no big demonstration.

The sheriff and the deputies were quietly asking friends of Darren what they thought of him and why anyone would want to kill him; especially in this manner.

There were no clues and nothing to give the sheriff the opportunity to arrest someone. He was getting discouraged. In the twenty-four years he had been in law enforcement, there had been only one other murder. There had been a lot of vandalism and annoying small crimes, but nothing this big.

Shickshinny was a small town of a little less than a thousand people. It was in Luzame County which was not all that big.

Three weeks went by and one day a deputy came with a citation for Kyle stating that he would probably be charged with the murder of Darren Kennedy. Kyle was taken in for questioning. When he arrived at the jail, Mr. Kennedy was there looking smug.

"Now farm boy. We'll be able to send you to prison for life. You people can not possible be as passive and forgiving as I've been told. You might as well confess. You were angry that my son got off without being charged and you can't do anything against him publicly. I think you waited to get your chance to get to him hoping you would not be suspected."

Kyle said nothing. He thought to himself '*A gentle answer turns away wrath, but a harsh word stirs up anger*. (Proverbs 15:1) He just stood saying nothing while Mr. Kennedy ranted and raved until he was red in the face and shaking. He looked as if he were going to attack Kyle at any minute.

Deputy Monroe Porter stepped between them. "Now Mr. Kennedy. No one has been charged with a crime yet. We're still working to find out what really happened. Why was your son killed and why was he taken to an Amish barn and left?"

Sheriff Fleming was sad to see that newspapers and television reporters were hanging around the town hoping to get a big story.

Kyle was questioned until he was confused and worried. Amos and Jacob were at the court house, but were not permitted to go in where Kyle was being questioned.

Joshua Kime joined them one day and told them something he had heard.

Angela Wilkins had been home from college but had to go back for an early session. It was common knowledge that she and Darren had dated and that Angela was crazy about him. Would she know anything?

The three men asked to speak to the sheriff and told him of the attraction between the two young people.

"Maybe she knows something that we haven't found out yet," Amos said hopefully. "Can you get her back here or could you send someone to talk to her?"

"I don't think I can get her back here, but I can send someone to talk to her. Come to think of it, she wasn't present at the funeral. She probably couldn't get away from college at that time."

Kyle was dismissed and allowed to go home. There was rejoicing in the home, but the dark cloud still hung over them.

There was continued harassment of anyone wearing Amish clothing.

A few loyal customers continued to shop at Amish owned stores, but business did suffer.

Sheriff Fleming was frustrated at the lack of clues or evidence in the death of Darren Kennedy. He had not been able to get in touch with Angela because she had gone to Spain with a college group. Finally the third week of August she had returned and come home for a short visit. She was shocked and appalled to hear of the death of a dear friend.

"I didn't know," she cried. "Oh, if I had only known that would be the last we would see each other I would not have been so angry at him."

"Why were you angry?" Sheriff Fleming asked.

"Darren had said we would get engaged before I returned to college. When we discussed it he said he was not sure he was ready for a commitment. He was the one who always talked of an engagement and made plans of marriage. I stupidly had told some of my friends at college that I would return with an engagement ring. I was embarrassed, hurt and, I guess, a little angry."

"Would you be kind enough to tell me what you did discuss?"

"There's not much more I can tell you. I did bake some banana nut muffins for him because he loved them so much. He ate two and drank a cup of coffee at my house and took six home with him. Knowing what a sweet tooth he has -- uh had, he probably ate them the same night."

The Sheriff drew back in surprise and with a frightening thought. "Do you remember what you placed in the muffins?"

"Yes, sir. I used a recipe my mother had always used. You can read the ingredients in her cook book."

"Please show it to me."

She took him into the kitchen and showed him the recipe in the book.

"And you used all of these ingredients?"

"Of course. Why do you ask?" She was puzzled.

"Angela, the Medical Examiner determined that he had ingested a large dose of rat poison possibly in muffins."

She shrieked. "We don't even have any of that in our house. I would certainly be too careful to use a poison of any kind."

"Calm down. I'm not accusing you. I'm only telling you what was found in his stomach."

"Oh, please. I hope you won't think I had something to do with his death. I would never be that cruel to anyone. Are you suspecting anyone?"

"He was found in an Amish barn; in fact in a barn of one of the young men he, and his buddies, had fought in town one day."

"That's something else we disagreed about. I told him I did not approve of what he did. I know the Amish would not lift a hand in anger against anyone. It's against their religion. Now what happens?"

Sheriff Fleming looked at her. "I'm going to continue to question his friends, if they are his friends, and hopefully someone will remember something they had thought was not important."

"Would you like for me to talk to them?"

"Oh, no. thank you, but this is police business." He started to go to the front of the house preparing to leave, but stopped and looked thoughtful.

"I would like for your parents to approve of your involvement, but as you're in their age group, maybe some of the young people would talk more freely to you than they would to us. If your parents approve, I'll get with you and give you some questions to ask."

"Please let me help. I'll do anything you say."

Before the Sheriff could talk to Angela's parents, there was another calamity in the Amish community. A tremendous thunder storm came up suddenly with powerful thunder and lightning.

The water back of Adam's filled and ran over the banks. People were keeping their children in for fear they'd get caught in the rising water.

There were two big cracks of thunder and several lightning flashes running horizontal across the sky. Then a big streak of lightning came down and hit the barn of Tobias Hershberger. He and his two oldest sons, Mordecai and

Joshua ran out to get the animals to safety. The hay and wood were burning rapidly. Tobias was burned on his back when a burning timber fell on him. Mordecai drug his father out and called his sister, Silvia, to come see to their father.

Tobias' wife, Marcella, had already rung the big bronze bell to alert the neighbors that there was trouble and they needed help. In spite of the weather, eight buggies, full of people were soon there to help any way they could. The women ran in to help prepare food for the workers if it was necessary.

Isaac Slabough shook his head. "There is no hope for the sheiyah, but all the gediere are safe."

Abraham Zook said, "There's nothing more we can do here until it stops raining. We always help each other. Don't worry." He patted Marcella's shoulder. "How is Tobias?"

"Danki for asking. He is burned but not too bad for me to put a salve on his back and keep his down for a few days." She shook her head. "That will be the hard part."

"Nee," Jacob laughed. "Keeping his out of his clothes for a few days will be the hard part."

"Ja, I may have to tie him down--- on his stomach."

No one wanted to eat, so soon the Hershberger family was alone.

On Sunndawk the service was held in the home of Benjamin and Angela Lapp. The Bishop reminded everyone of the Hershberger loss and said that there would be a barn raising on the following Deensdawk if it was dry enough. Everyone was thrilled to think of getting together with one of the few social events they had. They called it a frolic.

CHAPTER SEVEN

The day promised to be bright and clear, but humid and hot. August was holding the heat of the summer. An Englisch neighbor, David Bolling, was in the construction business. He offered a big truck and drivers to help haul any material needed. He also offered to furnish some picnic benches and tables for as long as they were needed to serve food.

Dr. Jonathan Alicea and his wife Catherine came to be available in the event there was an accident. He also had a tool belt on and was willing to work. Catherine was wearing brown slacks and a yellow blouse, but was willing to work with the women. Their sons, Conrad and Marshall, offered to do what they could. Would Catherine be accepted?

Catherine came hesitantly into the house carrying two hundred yeast rolls and two cakes she had baked. She was welcomed and put to work preparing vegetables for a stew.

By six O'clock, the yard held thirty some buggies and more than ninety boys and men were ready to go to work. Children from eight to twelve were given the task of bringing water and lemonade around often for the hot, tired workers.

Jacob took charge as he was the most skillful builder among them. He divided the men and older boys into four groups. Each group was to take a side of the barn and start building a frame for it. All of the Amish men were skilled in building because they did their own work. It was a very rare occasion when an outsider was needed.

On the previous Friday, concrete had been poured and pressure treated posts had been set in for supports. Adam, Matthew, Kyle, Gerry and Michael had taken the responsibility for this.

As the men worked someone would start singing a hymn. They would all join in. This really was joyful and entertaining for them. Musical instruments were forbidden in church, but Oliver Snader and Anthony Raber had sneaked harmonicas into their pockets. Nothing was said when they began to play. It wasn't a religious service, so Deacon Verkler decided it was all right.

The women were preparing fried chicken, beef and vegetable stew, ham and liver as well as a variety of salads, vegetables and more desserts than could surely be eaten. Everyone had breakfast at home before the day started. Lunch and dinner would be served on the Hershberger grounds.

By noon all four skeleton sides were completed. The skeleton framework was ready for lifting. Before the men were seated Deacon Verkler called for prayer. There was complete silence until he cleared his throat to show he was finished.

Younger teen girls brought out big baskets of hot yeast rolls. Butter, jams, and seasonings were already on the tables. Boys helped carry out the heavy baskets of food. The women, who had come to help, had brought china and tableware as well as food. Soon everyone was "eating themselves full" meaning eat all you want.

It is a good thing they were in the open because the sautéed onions to go with the liver were smelling mighty strong. Men joked about keeping the insects away from them as they ate liver and onions. The three big hams were cut at the tables. Mashed potatoes, potato cakes, pickled beets, green beans, asparagus, baked corn pudding, squash, zucchini, peas and slaw were a few of the vegetables served. Cakes, pies, puddings and homemade ice cream were desserts.

Dr. Alicea had worked as hard as any of the Amish. Fortunately all he had to do was treat splinters and a few cuts. He was impressed with the skill, friendliness, and dedicated work the people exhibited.

After the men had eaten, the women and children sat down to eat. Catherine Alicea was impressed with the welcome she had received and that she had been put right to work with the women. She could hardly wait to try some of the recipes she had collected.

The men rested for about a half hour and then went back to work. Half of them gathered on one side of the building to help raise the skeleton framework for the sides. The back and front did not require as much work because they would make doors another day. Also at the back was a big window over the door with a rope and a wench to lift heavy bales and any items to be stored in the loft.

There was some hammering, but, for the most part, round oak pegs with square heads were made to fit in holes and hold boards to the framework. Metal V shaped pieces had been purchased to hold the angled boards together for the loft.

All four sides had been filled in, but another day would find them working on the rafters. Then doors would be put in place and a shingle roof put on. A room had been built for storage of feed and tack. Stall partitions had been built in.

Thankfully the cow barn had not been damaged. While the men were working, the younger teen boys and girls were washing the kees udders and attaching the milking machine to each one. Each kee was eating while she was being milked.

It took three days in all and everyone was pleased with the work. The barn had even been painted by the teen boys.

On the third day, one of the men had slipped, while on the roof, and tumbled off. Thankfully he only had a broken arm. Dr. Alicea and his wife felt inspired while working with the people and he determined to be available whenever he was needed at a reasonable price for his services. He realized they had little money; only what they earned by selling things they had grown or made by hand. Sometimes the older teen and younger twenty boys, who were in Rumspringa, would work in town for a contractor or in some other business. They would give most of their pay to the parents.

As Dr. Alicea left he thanked the men for allowing him to be part of their working crew and told them how much he admired their fortitude and perseverance as well as their loyalty to each other.

Benjamin Lapp pulled his long full beard and said, "Ve mir lewe uff hoffning ue and Gott. (We live on hope and God.)"

"Forgive me if I'm out of line, but I do want to be your friend and I'm curious about some things. Why do you wear beards but no mustache?"

The Amish all looked to Deacon Verkle. "In the old countries, many years ago, our families were persecuted for being as they were. The soldiers wore full mustaches, therefore, we don't want to look like them. We follow Leviticus 19: 27 that states *Do not cut the hair at the sides of your head or clip off the edges of your beard."*

Dr. Alicea thanked them again and told Kyle he did not believe Kyle could be guilty of murder. "After what I have observed while working with all of you, I would even say you have all earned a place in Heaven."

Deacon Verkler then quoted Matthew 7:21 *Not everyone who says Lord, Lord will enter the kingdom of Heaven, but only he who does the will of my Father who is in Heaven.*

"I'm impressed with the way everyone helps all the rest and doesn't expect pay."

Joshua Kime said *Blessed is he who has regard for the weak; the Lord delivers him in times of trouble.* (Psalm 41:1)

"My goodness," Dr. Alicea looked startled, " you have a Bible verse for all conversations. Do all of you memorize them?"

"Ja," Jacob answered, *"I have hidden your word in my heart that I might not sin against thee."* (Psalm 119:11)

"I don't know what to say. I've been in church all of my life and have studied the Bible, but I'm ashamed to say, I have not memorized everything I studied. Well, we must be going. Thank you again for allowing me to be part of your work crew,"

Watching them go down the driveway, Charity said, "It's a crying shame that all Englisch are not as kind-hearted as Dr. and Mr. Alicea."

Jacob looked sternly at her. Charity had been speaking out more than an Amish woman should do. But then, he smiled to himself, she's more like me than any of the boys are.

Adam was so good working with wood and making animals. Charity asked him to teach her some of what he was doing.

"Charity, this is considered men's work. Why do you want to learn? I haven't wanted to tell you but the Bishop and the Deacon have talked to me about letting you be so free and get by with so much."

"What ?!" She stomped her foot. "How dare they accuse you of something I'm doing on my own. Oooo, I want to tell them off."

Laughing delighted, Adam hugged her and swung her around. "That's what they are talking about. You are too free to speak out with your thoughts. Amish women just don't do that. They let the men do the discussing and----"

"Too free! Do you mean to tell me I'm not permitted to think about anything and express myself?"

"Nee. It is just not seemingly for a woman to be so verbal in public. Talk to me all you want, but try to control yourself around others."

"What did you tell them?"

"I told them I had an intelligent, loving wife who excelled in cooking, sewing, keeping house and being a good Christian woman. I did not want to cause you any emotional pain to where you would stop thinking or talking to me. I think I confused them and left them wondering what kind of man I am." He laughed loud and long.

She spun around with her arms out. "Oh, Adam. I do love you and am so proud to be your wife. I think I made the best bargain to get you for a husband. Gott is gud."

"Ja. God is good, and I thank Him every day for what we have."

Each evening, before going to bed, they read from the Bible together and had prayer. "I can hardly wait to teach a little one from the Bible and our songs." Charity hugged herself and got a mellow look in her eyes.

"Ja. As the head of the house it will be my duty, and my pleasure, to teach our little ones. You can tell them stories from the Bible and teach them songs." He held one of their wedding presents, a family Bible.

Adam carefully placed the big, heavy Bible on the small table reserved for it. He turned to take Charity in his arms and hold her close. They finally held hands and went up to bed.

The next morning Charity was very thoughtful. "Adam, I'm worried that we have not heard any more about the death of that Kennedy man. Do you think his parents will have enough influence to declare Kyle guilty and put him in prison? I could not stand that for his family. It isn't common knowledge, but he has been escorting Michelle Lehann home after the singings and it sure looks as if they may be published. I hope and pray nothing keeps that from happening."

"I saw Deputy Glenn Woodward at the market last weekend. He said they are still talking to Darren's friends hoping some of them will remember something that will help solve the case."

"We are all praying for the truth to come out soon. Now how about showing me how to use your wood working tools."

"You are determined aren't you?"

"Yes. When the boppli comes I'll be kept indoors a lot, especially with winter coming on. I would love a hobby of making birdhouses."

He sighed loudly. "All right. Let me get my tools and some wood and I'll show you."

Charity waited anxiously while he got everything that would be needed.

"Now Charity, listen carefully. These tools are very sharp and can cause a very bad wound with careless handling. First I want to show you how they are to be used."

Adam spent about fifteen minutes telling her what each tool was and its purpose. Charity was artistic and she was sure she could do well. He then took a piece of wood and a broad-tipped pencil to lightly draw a design on it. "When you gain some experience, you won't have to draw the design first. You'll see the finished product in your own mind and can work on it."

By the end of a week Charity was doing well enough until Adam left her on her own. She was elated when she had the pieces for a birdhouse. After putting them together she did something she wasn't sure the Bishop would approve. She painted the house to look like an Englisch cottage.

"Charity! What are you doing?"

"Adam, the Englisch will mostly be buying these and I want to make them attractive for them. I'll make some for our Amish friends."

On the next Saturday that they went to town to an open market, Charity took ten of her birdhouses. Adam took some of his and three dog houses. They were pleased when they sold out soon after lunch. Charity wanted to walk around and see what others were selling and maybe find friends to talk to.

"We'd better not. We still don't know who killed the Kennedy boy or why he was placed in the Snader barn. The Bishop thinks it's to cause more trouble for us."

"Adam, that is so unfair. None of us did anything to cause the trouble and we have to be the ones being so careful."

"I know. It's better to be safe than sorry. Isn't that what your daed says?"

"Ja. I'm sometimes unhappy that we have to turn the other cheek."

"We need to live according to Gottes wille. (God's will)"

She sighed deeply. "Ja, I know, but sometimes it is awfully hard for me to turn away. It is even harder to forgive."

"I know my wunderbaar glatzkeppich (wonderful stubborn) wife. I naemlich do (love you). Remember, if we can't forgive how can we expect Gott to forgive us our sins?

"Ja. I know all of that and do believe. We'll teach all our kinner the same, but there are times that I feel we should do more to protect ourselves."

"Charity, my darling wife, that's for Gott to do. Protect us. If we talk about His will, but don't trust Him enough to take care of us, then we will be a failure as a community. Too, we are better witnesses to the Englisch if we follow His teachings and do as He wants us to do."

CHAPTER EIGHT

August twenty-seventh was rapidly approaching. It was Adam's birthday and Charity wanted to do something special for him and surprise him. He had said he was not accustomed to celebrating in his home which shocked Charity. Her family had always had a special dinner and a cake for the birthday person.

She first talked to her mother and her siblings who thought it was a great idea.

"Soon it will be weather too bad to get out much and you'll be having the boppli. I'll help all I can," Matthew assured her.

Matthew had been published to Deborah Yoder and planned for a late October wedding. He had already purchased a set of fine china for her as an engagement gift instead of a ring. Jacob and Moses had helped him acquire land near them and would help them build when the time was right.

"Mamm, I'm going to invite Sheriff Fleming and his wife to Adam's surprise party. In spite of all we can do, there will be a lot of talk and I have a feeling that some of the people from town may see this as an opportunity to do some damage by having a lot of us together."

Jenna Mae gave a deep sigh. "It seems to me that it is not Christian to be so suspicious of people."

"Mamm! I wouldn't call it suspicion; I say it is just being sensible and planning ahead, besides I have a funny feeling I can't explain."

"Ask your daed what he thinks about it. The Flemings are welcome, but for what reason?"

"Jenna Mae," Jacob thought carefully, "Charity may be right. We cannot be aggressive, but we can plan ahead and hope to avoid trouble. Of course the Flemings are welcome."

With careful hand, Charity wrote:

Mr. & Mrs. Fleming,

You are invited to a <u>surprise brithday</u> party on August 27, ----- at 3 PM at the home of Adam and Charity Kime. Please do not feel you have to bring a gift. Just attend and join in a family honor. Remember, this is to be a surprise to Adam.

RSVP

Charity Kime

Anita opened the envelope first and was astonished as well as thrilled. She knew it was unusual for people outside the Amish faith to be included in something so special to them. She could hardly wait for Micah to come home to share the news with him. She also had more good news. That morning their doctor had told her they would be expecting their first child. They had wanted to have children and had tried so hard for a little more than five years. She knew Micah would be floating with joy.

Micah hated to call Anita and tell her he could not come home for lunch. There was trouble with some unsubs (unknown subjects) stealing horses and sheep from the Amish. He hoped it would be soon that they found the guilty parties. He felt badly that the Amish were being harassed so much, and felt it wasn't fair since they could not strike back.

"Oh, Micah, I have such good news to share with you."

"Tell me now."

"No, my darling. I need to see you and share this good news with you."

"That's right. You had a doctor's appointment this morning. Does your good news involve your appointment? I hope it means you're in good health."

"I'm in perfect shape. Get home when you can. I love you. Stay safe."

"I adore you, my dear love. I'll stay safe for you."

Micah hurried out to join two deputies who were going the same direction. They felt that if they each took a section to look over, they might find the culprits, or at least some clues. They stayed in touch by radio.

Micah stopped at the farm where the family horses were stolen. Two little girls were crying so hard because their beloved horse was gone; they didn't know who had her or if she was being treated well. She was expecting a little one and they were afraid for her. The other two were geldings.

It broke Micah's heart to think of their grief and he became very angry at the stupidity and heartlessness of some people. He would never understand why the Amish were being treated so badly just because they were mild, passive people who bothered no one, paid their own way and expected no help from the government.

Two hours went by with the men keeping n touch by radio. Neither one had found anything helpful. In fact, they were getting upset at the attitude the people outside of the

Amish faith demonstrated. A few were sympathetic, but most of them said, "Good enough. Let them go live somewhere else with their farms and their animals."

Micah and the deuties wanted badly to remind them that the Amish furnished the milk, butter, honey, eggs, fresh vegetables, fruits and some meat that most of them depended upon.

Three hours had gone by and Micah and the deputies were beginning to think they would find nothing. Micah was just ready to radio the deputies and tell them to go on back to the station when one of them called him.

"Sheriff! Sheriff! I think I found some horses loose in a field. There doesn't seem to be anyone around that can tell me anything. The people who live nearby say they know nothing about the animals."

"Where are you, Glenn? Can you hear, Roy?"

"Yeah, I can hear. Go on, Glenn."

"Just on a hunch I went on 239 North to State Route 11. Just as I came on some people horseback riding on the Ssusquehanna Warrior Trail, I stopped them to ask if they had seen any horses. One woman said they were curious because there was a field full of nothing but brambles and weeds. They had never seen any horses in there before, but today there were three beautiful horses. The animals ran to the fence and nickered at them. They were thirsty and covered in stickers. They looked hungry and one even seemed to be scared. I rode in as far as I could and walked about an eighth of a mile and found them. They ran to the fence 'talking' to me."

"Stay with them. I'll call Jeb Turner to come get them. I'll notify the veterinarian Dr. Bussiere to meet us there. I'm coming as fast as I can. Roy, meet us there. We might need man power."

Glenn stayed with the horses and wished he was anywhere else but here. His heart ached for them. They walked the fence and begged him to release them, to feed them, to give them water. He knew what they wanted by the way they acted.

It took some time for Micah and Roy to join Glenn. Jeb was right behind them with his four horse trailer. Micah looked for a gate and couldn't find one, so, he cut the wire and peeled it back careful to not get barbs in him or the horses.

Jeb had some water that he divided among the three, but not enough to make them sick.

Dr. Jerome Bussiere came soon after to check the horses. "They aren't too bad, except for the pregnant mare. She is suffering trauma as well as lack of nutrition. Bring them to my clinic and I'll give them a thorough going over. Boy, this makes me angry. Micah, what can we do about this?"

Micah shook his head. "I'm angry, also. I know what I want to do, but it isn't legal or moral. I have a plan that I hope will work. Trust me, gentlemen. I'll tell you all about it as soon as I can."

Back at Jerry's Vet. Clinic, the horses were bathed, shots given, fed and taken care of. The family that owned them was notified. The stolen sheep and pigs still had not been found.

Esau Klopfenstein brought his children to see their horses. Ten year old Amelia and eight year old Louisa cried and hugged them, promising them that they loved them and would never let this happen to them again. The mare crooned over the little girls and showed her love for them.

Micah put his plan into action. He called each of the pastors and priests in Shickshinny and nearby and ask them to come to a very important meeting the following Saturday in his office. He also invited several newspaper reporters and television reporters.

Everyone came at ten in the morning for this meeting. They were curious as well as concerned. Micah had pastries, coffee, juice and water to offer.

They all talked among themselves for a few minutes while the reporters set up lights and necessary equipment.

Micah called for them to have a seat and allow him to talk. They listened carefully and courteously. "I need your help. All of you are aware of the harassment toward the Amish people and the cruelty done against them." He told them of the fight and of the death of Darren as well as the theft of the animals and other property.

"I thought the perpetrators would be satisfied and stop, but instead it has escalated. Their actions have now reached a very dangerous stage. I am truly afraid there will be more deaths and more property damage if we do not band together to put a stop to this."

"What do you want us to do?" Rev. Charles Barrington asked. "Darren's family are members of my church and I have come to the conclusion that there is no reasoning with his father. Don't you dare quote me and print that," he turned to the reporters. "It would damage my ability to reach him and reason with him. Please, think before you print something that could be inflammatory. They would think I had betrayed them and turned against them and that's not the truth. I care about all involved."

"I do, too," the other ministers spoke.

Father Herman Morgan of the Catholic Church stood up. "I've been very concerned because some of the young men that I suspect may be involved are from good homes and are members of my parish. At least they appear to be good homes," he said softly as he sat down.

Micah allowed them to talk among themselves for a few minutes and then spoke again. "I would appreciate it if all of you would pray about this and give a sermon or a talk about it during your services tomorrow. Select some Bible verses that fit the occasion and lay it on thick about compassion, caring for others and treating people as you would like to be treated. I don't object if you mention the cruel treatment to people and animals that has been going on."

"Could we talk about what the punishment might be, other than what God can levy against them? How about asking anyone who knows about this to come tell us?" one minister asked.

"That's fine with me," Micah answered, "however, we don't know for sure what the punishment might be. I can guess according to what has been done in the past."

"That's good enough for us," the Verizon FIOS reporter said. The news reporters from Suburban News and Citizen's Voice agreed.

"Well, I can say that there is a possibility of a thousand dollar fine and a year in jail for each animal stolen. Abuse would be a little more. I don't set the fines. It would all depend on what animal it was and what happened to them. The pregnant mare has been given the most abuse and I would expect more of a fine for her."

"That satisfies us. We'll print the story about the senseless actions and hopefully put the fear of God in anyone who would participate or encourage such a crime." All the reporters agreed.

"I can hardly wait to get home and prepare my sermon. I hope to put the fear of God in anyone who is guilty or knows who is responsible for the crime." Several ministers voiced the same plan.

Micah thanked them for coming and asked that they feel free to contact him at any time.

As the ministers were leaving the Catholic priest turned. "I'm in a bind. If someone tells me this in confession, I can't talk about it. How can the rest of you bring the story public if someone comes to you to confess?"

Rev. Barrington placed a friendly hand on the shoulder of the priest. "We are to do God's will and He plainly tells us that we **are** our brothers' keeper. We are to protect anyone whether they are a member of our church or not. At the same time, we can only appeal to their moral and spiritual side and entreat them to come forward on their own."

The breaking news on television that night carried the story of the stolen horses and showed the little girls crying their hearts out. They also told of the fight and other harassment and ended by saying, "We know we can't like everyone we meet, but then everyone doesn't have to like us. We are supposed to be civilized people and get along together. I spoke to a teacher, Mrs. Sioux Stallard and she said that a flower garden was beautiful because of all the different colors and types of plants. She went on to say that our nation is beautiful because of the different colors of people and different backgrounds. We need to appreciate and accept even if we don't mix with them.

The Sunday papers carried the same story in more detail and more pictures. The story also included the murder of Darren Kennedy and ended by asking anyone who knew anything to come forward. They ended by encouraging people to talk to any minister whether they attended that church or not. If they wished they could talk to Sheriff Fleming at any time. If they wished to remain anonymous, that could be arranged.

Micah and Anita prayed together and ask that someone have a guilty conscience and talk to someone. Micah was ready to cry for the people who were being abused and tormented. "Annie, I hope and pray someone will give us something to go on after this weekend."

"Pray without ceasing, my darling. Thank God for **our** precious news and tell Charity that we'll be delighted to attend Adam's surprise party. I'm going to make a gallon of hot German Potato Salad and a gallon of coleslaw. They don't expect us to do anything but show up, but I want to be part of the festivities. Are you going to get a gift for him?"

"I don't know. If others don't bring one it might make them resent me."

"I didn't think of that. Maybe you can do something for him on the sly."

CHAPTER NINE

The week slowly drifted by with no more trouble and no one coming forward. Thursday was Adam's party. He would be twenty-one.

Charity was like a worried chicken, running all over the place and worrying about the day not going well. How could she get Adam out of the field and cleaned up in time?

Jacob came to the rescue. "Adam, there's a horse auction at the fair grounds. I'd appreciate it if you would go with me and look at the horses. Can you be ready to leave at one?"

"Ja. I guess I can spare the time. I planned to do some wood work, but I'm caught up on personal orders. Ja, I'll go."

Jacob drove the buggy up the driveway at a few minutes before one. Adam had a good lunch and a fresh bath. He was ready to go after he hugged Charity and kissed her urging her to rest some.

They were no more than out of sight until buggies came in. Two trucks and a car of auslanders (outsiders) came in also. The buggies were parked behind the barn and the horses turned loose into the field back of the house. The trucks and car were parked back of the house. Then men started setting up tables and benches and the women got all the food together. Some had brought extra china and tableware.

Micah and Anita worked with them and were relieved when no one even looked questioningly at them. Jonathan and Catherine Alicea had been invited as were David and Victoria Bolling.

There were no balloons or any frills such as would be found at a party in the home of an outsider. Just good food and good company. There was coffee, lemonade, cider and water for beverages.

The food was too numerous to list as Adam was well-liked and everyone was delighted to have an excuse to get together in fun.

Bishop Eash and his family were present as were the two ministers Joshua Chupp and his family, Jude Nissley and his family and Deacon Moses Verkler and his family. Seventy-four were present in all.

Adam was certainly surprised as they drove up and saw the crowd. At first he had a lump in his throat thinking something was wrong, then he had a big grin when Charity ran to him and everyone shouted, "Hallich gebottsdaag!"

Harmonicas were produced when the singing started. Singing was something they all enjoyed doing. No musical instruments were allowed for fear they would appear worldly, but since this was a social gathering, and not a worship service, nothing was said about the harmonicas being played. A lot of the singing was done in their own language so the auslander guests could not participate, but they did truly enjoy them.

The food was soon demolished, but they waited awhile for dessert. Deacon Verkler surprised them by getting up and asking anyone to tell about a birthday they remembered, especially the older folks. There was a little sadness, but the majority of the stories were funny and enjoyable.

Micah had them laughing when he told of a birthday he remembered on his Grandfather's farm when he was eight. "I had wanted my own horse as badly as any child can want a horse. I begged, promised and pleaded, but no one would tell me if I was getting a horse. Finally my big sister said what I was getting was white and red. I was so sure it was the pinto I had my heart set on. I unwrapped the gifts thinking the horse would surely be outside. Finally I unwrapped some white shirts and red overalls. I tried very hard not to cry. I threw the clothes on the floor and stomped out yelling, "How am I going to ride clothes?" My little heart was broken when everyone laughed at me. Now I think it's funny, but I'll never do that to a child of mine."

Micah turned to his wife. "Sweetheart, may I tell them our good news?" She nodded. He turned with his chest out and said, "We've tried for about six years to have a child and last week the doctor told us we could expect a child next May. Yipppeee!"

They all laughed with him and clapped to show their approval.

Finally the women brought out several big, beautifully decorated cakes with home made ice cream. It was a beautiful ending to a lovely day. The people were getting ready to leave when Micah's cell phone rang. He apologized and walked closer to the house to listen. He returned looking angry.

"A car ran a horse and buggy off the road where the buggy turned over. The horse had to be put down because of serious injury. The people are in Mercy Hospital and they are Amish. The man is in critical condition." He turned to his wife, "Honey, can we take their three children for the time being? I don't know yet who their relatives might be."

"Of course we'll take the children. You didn't even have to ask."

"Wait," Bishop Eash said. "Who is it? We may know the relatives."

"I doubt it. They are from another town. My deputy said the woman gave her name as Rebecca. They have three small children."

"It is kind of you to be willing to help, but the Amish take care of their own. We'll take the children and the woman, if necessary."

"Ja." Several families came forward to offer to do what they could.

Micah stood thoughtfully. Would you, or a couple of men, be willing to ride in my car with me and see about them. Then I'll bring you and the children back to wherever you wish to go."

The church leaders stood in a group with some of the men of the church. Noah Kime came to Micah. "I'll go with you and do whatever is necessary."

Charity put her head on her dad's shoulder and cried. "I had a feeling something bad would happen. Maybe I shouldn't have planned the party."

Jacob lightly shook her. "You having the party had nothing to do with it. The careless driver of the car is at fault. We'll all have to pray for him as well as the injured family."

Noah got in Micah's car with Anita and they drove to Mercy Hospital. In the waiting room they found a woman crying piteously. When she saw them come into the room, she turned her shoulder away from them and tried to stifle her sobs.

Noah walked over and, in the language, introduced himself and said the Amish community was ready and willing to help. The lady looked up at him with beautiful azure blue eyes filled with tears, but could not talk for a few moments.

"Mine Clint, he is hurt so bad. I am so sad that I cannot pray."

Micah and Anita walked over and Anita sat down to place an arm around the woman. "We are ready and willing to help also. If you feel to upset to pray, may I pray? The woman looked at her and then at Noah. He nodded. She said, "Ja, danki."

Micah knelt on his knees and took the woman's hand. Noah hesitated and then knelt beside Micah and took her other hand.

Anita prayed. "Lord, You are the Heavenly Father of all of us. We may choose to worship in different ways, but we believe in you and in your promises. You have said you will never give us more than we can live with.

You also said You would never leave us. We humbly ask that you lay Your loving arms around Clint and heal him so that he can be with his family who loves him and needs him. Be with his family and give them courage to face the future and to be at peace knowing all that happens is God's will. We thank you for loving us and being with us when we need you."

Micah said, "Amen," and then stood. Noah looked interested, but questioning and said nothing.

"I have never heard a prayer like that, but I like it. My name is Purity Kime."

"Kime!" Noah said and then spoke more softly. My name is Noah Kime. My family and my brothers and sisters all live here in our community. We must talk and determine if we are related."

At that moment a nurse came in with the three children. She had taken them out for ice cream and to give their mother some quiet time.

"Here are our children," Purity smiled with true motherly love. "Charity is ten, Jacob is seven and Amos is three. I don't know what we would do without them." Charity told her of the familiar names.

Noah greeted the children. "All of you are coming home with me until your daed can come with us. He will be here in the hospital for a little while and will be well cared for. I have big children at home, but they will be so happy to see you."

"Is mamm coming, too?" Jacob timidly asked.

"Ja, all of you. And daed will join you later."

Purity cried for happiness. "I wasn't sure how I was going to find a place to stay and feed my children. Thank you all so much," she turned to Anita.

Anita hugged her again. "Maybe you'll find relatives here. Anyway you'll find a lot of good friends who care and want to help. My husband and I will help, also."

Purity shyly took Anita's hand. "I've never had Englisch friends, but I am so glad to find you."

Micah put everyone in his car and took them to Noah's house. Noah's wife, Marilyn came out to meet them with open arms. "Kumme. Food is on the table. Sitz and eat yourselves full." She herded the children in while Noah, Micah and Anita talked outside.

"Micah, I can't thank you enough. Our people trust you and know you love the Lord as much as we do. I want to help in any way that I can to find the people responsible for the troubles in our community."

"Thank you, Noah. We'll work together on this and pray that the troubles will end very soon." Micah and Anita left, then Noah went into his house.

The next service was held in the home of Abraham and Christine Zook.

Bishop Eash told the people of the guests of Noah and urged everyone to make them welcome.

During the week, children's clothes, women's clothes, food, money and other items appeared at Noah's house without anyone claiming attention.

In three days, Clint was able to join his family, but had to rest a lot.

During the conversation of families, Noah found that Clint had lost his means of income and was hoping to find employment and a life in Shickshinny. Clint, a skilled worker, made furniture and other items of wood. They also discovered that Clint was the son of one of Noah's favorite cousins.

An elderly Swartley family had to go live with a daughter in another part of the state. They had left behind an empty house in good condition. Noah contacted them and got permission for Clint's family to live there until they could buy the property. There were eighty acres of excellent farm land and all the necessary buildings on the property.

Member of the community brought two milk cows, two mules, a plow, a buggy and a horse, several chickens, two pigs and feed for the animals. Different ones, women and men, came when they could and helped with the plowing, planting, putting in a flower garden and sharing canned goods already prepared for winter. Everyone pitched in to help.

Micah spread the word and various town people offered transportation, food, items needed for farming and best of all employment for Clint in the furniture factory in town. Neighbor boys Amish and Englisch helped with the farm work and many ways they were needed.

Micah and Anita were sincerely thankful. "Wouldn't it be wonderful if all of us, Amish and outsiders, could be together like this all of the time? I will never be able to understand where the hate and need to hurt take precedence over peaceful living. It seems to me that the guilt of doing something you know is wrong would be hard to live with."

Micah snorted. "The truth is they don't think they're doing anything wrong. Generations teach the following generations to hate or distrust because of color, nationality or religion. No, it doesn't make sense, but we'll have this to contend with as long as there are humans on this earth."

September rolled in and Charity began to wish the time would fly by. She had loved being pregnant and wanted children, but this bloated feeling, swollen feet and being tired most of the time was getting to her.

She had canned more than eight hundred jars of vegetables, fruits, jams, jellies and gallons of cider. She has also put up dozens of jars of grapes and juice to be mixed with ginger ale for a beverage. She was looking forward to the middle of the week when the community would get together to make apple butter and can more apples with spices.

Adam was in the process of killing hogs to make sausage, head cheese, and scrapple. The hams were to be processed and smoked, pork loins cut and ribs cut to be barbequed and shared with neighbors as they gathered for a fall festivity.

Adam had helped Charity prepare a room for the much awaited, already loved baby which would be here in a few weeks. He had made a swinging cradle, a stroller and a bassinet. If they had known the horrors that would follow, they would not have wanted to rush through the month.

CHAPTER TEN

A couple of the town ministers called Micah to say that they thought they were on the verge of getting some talk going. One minister had gone to a teen meeting and urged the teens to take action before they might be on the receiving end of harassment.

He told them, "If a person is mean-hearted enough to do these despicable things to an innocent person, think what they can do to you if they decide you are no longer their friend. You can't trust people like this."

Two girls had come to him and ask what would happen to a person who knew what was going on and told about it. He talked to them for several minutes, but they didn't have anything else to say.

Eight more days passed and Rev. Barrington called Micah. "My daughter, Tiffany, would like to talk to you. She's fifteen and mature for her age, but I want to be with her." Micah assured him it would be fine.

The next day, on a Tuesday, Tiffany and her father came to the station.

"Hello, Tiffany. My, you're getting to be a young lady. I can remember when you used to toddle by here and wave at all of us. You reminded me of a little Shirley Temple with your sweet dimples and curly hair." Micah truly was glad to see her and tried to make her feel at ease. "Please, come into my office and have a seat. Would you like a soft drink?"

"No, thank you Sheriff. I guess you know how nervous I am about coming here, especially when I feel I'm tattling on friends." Tiffany spoke softly.

"It isn't tattling when you're telling the truth about damage done to innocent people. Your age group probably sees it as such, but think of it as serving your country in bringing justice."

Rev. Barrington sat by Tiffany. "Don't be nervous, darling. The Sheriff is our friend and is trying to protect all of us. He can only do his job when citizens cooperate."

Micah leaned back in his creaky leather chair and placed his hands behind his head in a relaxed manner. "Just start wherever you wish and tell me whatever you think I should know. Do you object if I have one of the ladies take notes? I want to be positive I'm remembering the facts."

She looked at her father and he nodded his head. "I don't mind."

Micah flipped a switch on the office communicator and asked for one of the ladies to come in with a note pad and prepare to take a statement.

Ellen Mercer came in, smiled at them and seated herself beside Micah's desk and facing Tiffany. "I'm ready whenever you are," she smiled.

Tiffany took a deep breath and coughed. "I wasn't present at any of the occurrences and was not involved, but you know how kids talk. Some times it is the truth and some times it's bragging. Darren Kennedy didn't have a steady girlfriend, but he did date a lot. Ashley Wilkins has been going with Trudy Morton and Trudy loves to brag and talk. She thought it was hysterically funny about the boys harassing the Amish. Abner Washington is from a prominent family and thinks he's too good for any of us. He and Darren have apparently been the ring leaders in planning and encouraging the actions." Here she paused and asked for a drink of water.

"I'm sorry for what happened to Darren, but I don't think he was murdered."

"He wasn't?" Micah asked in surprise. "What do you think happened then because he's sure dead?"

"From what I've heard Ashley and Trudy say he did it to himself."

"How can that be?"

I agreed to go to the movies with Liam McDonald one night. Ashley, Trudy, Denver Whitmore and Lisa Cornett were with us. After the movie we went to the Pizza Hut for pizza and soft drinks. I couldn't be sure, but I truly think Ashley and Denver were high on something, but it wasn't alcohol. Trudy giggled and encouraged them to tell what they were going to do next to the Amish. During the telling Denver said it was a shame that Darren had been so stubborn. I asked him how he was stubborn. He answered that Darren thought he could live through anything. He had said some religions handled poisonous snakes and drank poison and he bet the stupid Amish did and he could do the same. Liam made them shut up and got up to leave. I had to go with him so I didn't hear any more than that. I had the feeling that Liam knew what was going on even if he wasn't involved."

Rev. Barrington stopped his daughter to ask her some questions. "Was that the only time you heard them talking about anything?"

"No, another time I was in the library at school and Trudy and Lisa came in and sat by me. Soon Linda Holden joined us. She has been dating Alan Barkley. Trudy started her giggling and whispered that she knew something exciting. We left before we got into trouble and went out in the courtyard.

We sat down at a stone table and bench by some hedges and talked quietly. The others were eager to talk and share stories and I just listened, feeling guilty the whole time." She looked at her father. "My parents have always told me to not indulge in gossip and not to repeat it, but I was curious."

She took a long drink from the bottle of cold water. "Trudy told us that she heard Ashley and Denver brag about stealing animals that belonged to the Amish. She also told us that Abner was bragging about his daddy running some of the crazy Amish off the road and wrecking their buggy."

Micah was flabbergasted. He could hardly wrap his mind around the fact that teens could be so cruel and brag about it. "Tiffany, do you really think Abner's daddy did run the buggy and horse off the road or was he just spouting off? The man almost died. The horse was killed and the buggy damaged so badly it was of no use. The family was left destitute. Thanks to the Amish community, they are being cared for."

"I don't know for sure, Sheriff. I'm just repeating what was told in my presence. Daddy said I couldn't even swear to it on a witness stand because it was -- what did you say daddy?"

"Hearsay. That means you don't know it yourself, you've just heard others talking."

"Tiffany, do you have anything else to share? I can tell you, honey, you've been an answer to prayer. What these boys are doing is not only mischief, but dangerous and could cause them to spend years in prison. They have not only damaged property, caused emotional hurt and annoying actions, but they've also put lives in danger. One of the horses that was stolen is a mare having a baby. She was in a lot of trauma besides being kept without food or water."

Tiffany began to wipe tears from he eyes. "I don't want to get them in trouble, but it isn't right what they're doing."

"Honey, they got themselves in trouble. I feel the parents are to blame for not training them better at home and not keeping in touch with them. Did your parents raise you thinking it was okay to damage property and place lives in danger?"

"Oh, no. My parents' hearts would be broken if they thought I was doing such things. I have not only been taught better, but I would have a guilty conscience and not like myself if I did such things."

"Honey, it isn't just because your father is a minister that you've been taught better, but as parents they've tried to raise a responsible lady."

Ellen stood up. "If that is all, do you mind if I go type this up and you can sign it before you leave here."

Rev. Barrington stood. "We'll wait. I'm so proud of my daughter for having the courage to talk to her mother and me and then come in here. She has told the truth, but I hope the other teens will not find that she has talked. I'm sure they would cause all kinds of grief for her and for us."

"I can assure you nothing will go out from this office. My staff knows that if they talk out of turn, they will be fired and I can get rough with people I can't trust." Micah assured them.

Ellen was soon back and handed Micah the papers. He rapidly read through them and gave them to Tiffany. "You and your dad read this and then, if you are satisfied, sign it, please." He walked out of the room to give them privacy.

Tiffany and her dad walked out and gave Micah the papers. "We're satisfied and hope this will help." Rev. Barrington said.

"I can't thank you enough. Tiffany, don't be fearful. No one here will talk about your statement and no one will even tell you've been in. If you parked in the lot behind here, would you like to go out the back door and then you won't be seen leaving."

Micah called Ellen in to take a letter. He handed her a list of names:

Burleigh and Mary Wilkins -- son Ashley
Thomas and Ellie Washington -- son Abner
James and Nicole McDonald -- son Liam
Richard and Hillary Whitmore -- son Denver
Brad and Bonnie Barkley -- son Alan
Marshall and Terry Morton -- daughter Trudy
Earl and Ellen Cornett -- daughter Lisa
Willis and Constance Holden -- daughter Linda
Charles and Charlene Barrington -- daughter Tiffany

"Write the same letter addressing one to each of these people. Tell them I am looking forward to meeting with them On Tuesday, September 11 at 3PM to discuss important affairs. Don't invite and don't leave it open for them to refuse. I want each of them here and no excuses."

"Do you mean to include the Barringtons? Won't the girls be suspicious of Tiffany being here?"

"No. It will be just the opposite. If they're all included the rest of them will not be suspicious. They'll just think I have something on all of them. I'll call Rev. Barrington and explain it to him and tell him to tell Tiffany to be low key."

Micah very carefully made notes so that he would not forget something. He and Anita prayed about it and he hoped this would bring an end to the Amish harassment.

The teens called each other and met wondering what the Sheriff wanted with them. None of them had an idea.

Abner strutted around. "If I find that somebody has squealed on us, I'll make them sorry they were born."

Tiffany was in tears telling her parents what was said. They assured her that none of the others knew she had talked to the Sheriff and if she kept calm and appeared as curious as the others, none of them would even consider her.

CHAPTER ELEVEN

Tuesday morning of September 11 opened with a cool rain which had ceased by noon. The air was chilly but the sun was out.

Everyone came on time except the Washingtons. They came in seven minutes late. Thomas walked into the conference room demanding, in a loud voice, to know what the *#^* was so important to call them out on a working day. No one answered him. He fumed for a few minutes and finally sat down. Ellie looked embarrassed, but said nothing.

Micah let them stew for a few minutes and then walked slowly in followed by Deputies Roy Braun and Glenn Woodward and Ellen Mercer. Ellen quietly took a seat near the back of the room and prepared to take notes. Roy and Glenn spoke to everyone and then sat near the door.

Thomas Washington loudly demanded to know why they were being inconvenienced in this manner. Micah ignored the outburst and stood in front of the group leaning against a stand.

"I want to first welcome all of you and thank you for being so prompt to respond. This is your home county and I know you're all concerned about the safety of all citizens which includes all of you."

Thomas started to spout off again, but Ellie put a hand on his arm and shook her head. From the expression of his face, Micah knew she would pay for her action when they returned home.

"As all of you know, I'm sorry and sad to say, we have some cowards living among us. These cruel, evil persons will not operate as an individual, but must have a group to support them and give them courage to do their evil deeds." There was silence.

Micah continued. "I'm talking about the evil cowards who harass innocent people and do damage to property. They also steal from people and were just short of committing murder. I'm talking about the horse and buggy that were run off the road. The horse lost his life and the buggy was damaged. The man was in critical condition almost leaving a wife and three little children, and I mean little children."

Burleigh Wilkins looked up from where he had dropped his head. "That was some of our people?"

"It was our people who elected to try to kill an innocent family rather than live and let live."

"What makes you think he intended to kill them?" Thomas spoke belligerently.

"I didn't say it was a man driving. It could have been a woman."

Thomas dropped his shoulders and settled back in his chair.

"We do have some clues pointing to that guilty party. I'm hoping he will come forward on his own and make it easier on himself. He will be facing a prison term and maybe a considerable fine. That will be up to the judge."

"Why would he be sent to prison for getting rid of someone that none of us want around?"

"Why would you, Mr. Washington?"

There was a deadly silence. Brad Barkley looked around. "If it is one of us, please tell us. We don't approve the methods at all. I don't particularly care to deal with the Amish, not because they have done anything I don't approve of. Taking a good look at myself, I probably feel threatened by them because they live such a good, clean spiritual life and make the rest of us feel guilty."

"Guilty!" Richard Whitmore said. "Why would you feel guilty? I sure don't. I've done nothing to feel guilty about." He looked at Micah. "Oh, I guess I have. Even though I haven't done anything directly against them, I haven't tried to talk others into leaving them alone. But I will. As of this day I promise that I will endeavor to be friendly and helpful."

Thomas clapped his hands sarcastically. "Rah for you. Do you think that's going to get you into Heaven?"

"No. I know what will get me into Heaven. I'm thankful for the life I've been privileged to live and all the blessings I have."

"Such as?"

"I have a wonderful wife, children who would make any parent proud, a good job, shelter, food and all necessities. I can truthfully say I have never done anything deliberately against anyone that would be hurtful."

James McDonald had been listening closely. "This is all interesting, but why are we here Micah? I have a feeling you haven't touched the surface yet."

Micah looked sternly around the group. "I have it by good authority that these boys and girls have been involved in the skullduggery going on. Some of you stole the animals and put their lives and health in danger. Some of you have harassed the Amish and made life miserable for them. All of those make you subject to a fine and could mean a jail term."

Mary Wilkins gave a little gasp. "Well my son is not involved. He's been taught better at home."

"I hate to be the one to burst your bubble, Mrs. Wilkins. But it is my understanding that Ashley and Darren Kennedy have been the ringleaders. They have made the plans and urged others to get involved."

"That's a lie!" Ashley yelled. "Anyone who says I was involved in any of it is a liar."

Trudy Morton moaned and placed her hand over her mouth.

"Trudy, has your big mouth been at work. Did you tell lies on me?"

She shook her head still covering her mouth and then tears started rolling down her cheeks.

Terry Morton quickly hugged her daughter. "Trudy, if you know anything about what's been going on, please tell us. Oh, it would break my heart if I knew you had done any of these cruel things."

Trudy sobbed. "No, mom. I haven't been involved, but I know who has and I've laughed with them and haven't tried to stop them."

"Shut up, b----," Abner yelled standing and making fists at his sides.

"Young man, you will not use language like that here and you will never talk to a young lady like that. After listening to your father this morning, I'm not surprised at your reaction. Why would you assume she was talking about you? She didn't name anyone."

"Are you saying I'm a bad person?" Thomas stood belligerently and walked toward Micah with his hands made into fists. Both deputies stood and moved closer. Micah motioned with one hand for them to wait.

"I haven't accused anyone and no names have been made known. Are you feeling guilty?"

"No, I'm not. Ask Bonnie Barkley what she knows. I know for a fact that she caught Alan and others talking about what they had done and, as far as I know, she has never reported it." He smirked.

"Mr. Washington, you are no gentleman. I'm not surprised that your son is involved, in fact a ringleader," Nicole McDonald spoke out. "We have been suspicious that our son knows about these incidents, but he hasn't talked about it. I think you should look at the girls our sons have been dating. Girls are more likely to talk among themselves."

Linda Holden started sobbing. "I'm so ashamed. Yes, I knew some of the things going on and some who were involved. But I didn't say anything and I'm so sorry. Sheriff, I'd like to tell you what I know."

Richard Whitmore, Burleigh Wilkins and Thomas Washington all jumped up at once trying to speak. Micah got them quiet and settled,

"That is the reason you're here. I have been told of the people and the events that have occurred and plans for the future. None of you here have been willing to come forward, so I had to bring you together." He looked at everyone, even the Barringtons but did not let on that they knew anything.

Micah continued. "I do know all the young people involved in the disgraceful fight on the Main Street. I've also been told the name of the man who ran the horse and buggy and family off the road. That's attempted murder. What I want to know Abner, were you the one who killed Darren Kennedy?"

"NO! No one killed Darren. He killed himself. We just hid him."

"Ellen, are you taking notes?"

"Yes, sir."

"Abner, please, tell us how Darren killed himself."

"We were all drinking and smoking pot that night. Darren came in with the muffins that his girlfriend had baked. We were talking about what all had been done to the Amish and they still hadn't left our county. We started making fun of their religion. Daren said he bet they even handled poisonous snakes and drank poison like some religions did. He then said he bet he could eat poison and survive like they did. He took some roach poison that my mom had to put out and he broke open the little boxes. He cut the muffins apart and put a big amount of the roach poison on the muffins. He dared us to eat with him, but none of us would, so he ate them all. I guess the alcohol and drugs didn't mix well with the roach poison."

Hillary said in a shocked voice. "And you just left him laying there and didn't ask for help or report it?"

"No," Abner continued, "we got scared and then we thought how funny it would be to blame his death on the

Amish. We carried him to my car and took him out there and left him in the barn. It was about three in the morning."

Micah said softly, "Abner, who is we?"

Abner looked beaten for the first time. "Ashley Wilkins, Alan Barkley, and Marshall Porter. We made a pact to never tell. I did finally tell my father and he told me to keep my mouth shut and be careful."

"Ellen, make a note to get Marshall Porter and his parents in here. In fact," he turned to Roy, "please go out and see if you can call them now. Tell them it's vitally important that they be here with Marshall."

Roy left to make the call and Glenn moved closer to Micah. Ellen continued to use shorthand and take down all comments.

"While we're waiting, I'd like to know who stole the animals and put the pregnant mare at risk. Where are the sheep and pigs?"

Abner looked around, perspiring heavily and not looking so arrogant. "Ask Denver Whitmore and Douglas Winthrop."

"Okay, the Winthrop family need to be brought in. Thank you Abner. It would have been better if you young people had never started any of this. It would have gone easier on you if you had come in on your own and told me of your involvement. I had to hear the gossip from your school friends."

"Who were they?" Thomas Washington demanded. "We have a right to face our accusers."

"You would have the right if you were innocent in order to protect yourselves, however, a judge will see it differently. By the way, I'm placing you under arrest now for the attempted murder of the Kime family and of the destruction of their horse and property. There were three little children and a woman at risk also in that buggy."

Glenn was behind him with cuffs before he could make a move. Still he fought and cursed as he was led out to be booked. Ellie had collapsed in tears. Abner paid no attention to his mother. His father had not given him the example of being kind to his mother or any woman.

James McDonald called, "Abner. Please tell me the truth. Was my son, Liam, involved in any of your cruelty?"

"No. Not involved, but he did listen to us talk and said nothing about it."

"Thank God. His mother and I have tried to set a good example and have taken him and his sisters to church all their lives. I still feel he needs a long talk with us and maybe with the pastor."

The girls were given a stern lecture about knowing what was going on and listening to the boys, but not telling anyone about it. They were warned that they could be considered guilty after the fact. Micah told them.

The boys were being held for Juvenile Court since they were all sixteen and seventeen. Micah answered the parents' questions the best he could.

He kept reminding them that the judge would decide what would be done with them. He did tell them there would probably be heavy fines and maybe even a year in Juvie. In any case, they would all have a police record.

Micah drove to the farm of the Snaders to tell them all concerning the death of Darren Kennedy and why he was left in their barn. Amos shook his head sadly and said, "We followed the will of Gott. *Cast your cares on the Lord and He will sustain you. He will never let the righteous fall, but You, oh God, will bring down the wicked.* (Psalm 55:22-23)"

"I'm so impressed with your love of God and your following His Word. It would be so much more pleasant if everyone did. I also admire all of you for being able to forgive and not holding a grudge," Micah said.

Amos tilted his head to one side, "*Jesus said, You have heard it said, love your neighbor and hate your enemy, but I say love your enemies and pray for those who persecute you that you may be the sons of your Father in heaven.* (Matthew 5: 43-44) If we did not forgive we cannot expect Gott to forgive us our sins. To hold a grudge is to not trust that Gott will take care of everything."

Micah returned home humble and thanking God for his friendship with the Amish. He knew they were human just like everyone else. There were rare cases where a man might be abusive to his wife and too harsh with his children. A man might be accused of rape. When any of that happens they are brought before the church which takes care of their own punishment.

Pastor Chupp informed the congregation on Sunday of the outcome of Micah's investigation. They were all relieved it was over and expressed their appreciation for Micah and those who were upholding the law.

Rev. Barrington talked to the Kennedy family and reminded them that the only person guilty of their son's death was their own son. They should stop blaming others and set a good example before their other children. "Hate only hurts the person who is doing the hating, especially if there is no need for it," he told them. He left feeling as if he had made no headway.

It was so quiet and peaceful that Micah began to have an itch in his stomach. He was afraid the English would not give up so easily. He was right.

CHAPTER TWELVE

On the morning of September 22, Charity rang the bell to call Adam in from the field. He came running, leaving the three neighbor boys to finish the work and take care of the animals.

"Adam, my water just broke. It is a little early, but I think our boppli is trying to join our family."

He was so nervous he could hardly harness Bonnie Kate and get the buggy ready to rush to town with Charity to Mercy Hospital. They had agreed that, instead of a midwife, they would go to the hospital with this first one.

"Do you want me to ask the Morrrisons to take us in their car and get there quicker," he asked nervously.

"No," Charity laughed, "I do not yet feel any pressure. You might slow down going past the Raber farm and ask them to tell my parents."

Bonnie Kate could feel Adam's concern and was dancing in the harness.

"Easy, pretty girl. You're pulling a precious load here. We count on you to get us to town safely."

Charity had to slow him down. He started out running. "Adam! Please slow down. You'll break Bonnie's leg and we have time. Don't get her so worked up."

As they were even with the Raber driveway, Adam yelled and Rosemary ran down to see what the excitement was. He talked so fast that Charity had to lean over and say, "I'm having the boppli. We're on our way to the hospital."

"Wonderful!" Rosemary said. "I'll send Anthony to tell your parents."

Adam had just started out again when they heard an angry horn behind them. Adam pulled over to allow the car to pass. The driver kept blowing the horn and yelling out the window at them. As he passed Bonnie, he cut toward her and blew his horn loudly. She reared and jerked to the side where she lost her balance and fell in the ditch.

Bonnie Kate's screams matched those of Rosemary as she ran toward them yelling loudly for her father. She had not noticed that Adam had been thrown out head first and the right rear tire of the car had run over him. Charity was barely hanging on to the side of the buggy and crying. Bonnie Kate was still screaming.

Deputy John Lynn happened along a minute later. He called for an ambulance and helped Charity out of the overturned buggy. Rosemary and her mother, Genevieve, carried Charity to the house. Gerry was sent running for the midwife.

The ambulance arrived before the midwife could get there, so the decision was made to take Charity to the hospital. She was in labor pains and not really caring just as long as she got some relief.

John let the ambulance go with Charity and Rosemary before he told the Rabers that Adam had died. He had landed head first on the concrete. Bonnie Kate had to be put down because she had two broken legs and internal injuries.

Jonathan was upset. "It is gud that Adam does not know. He loved his wife and he really loved that mare. He planned on breeding her next time around. I must tell Bishop about this. He and his wife will want to be with Charity."

Jonathan saddled a horse to ride over and tell the Bishop about the happenings. Rosemary had told him the Englisch man had yelled, "Why don't you go somewhere else and live. We don't want you here."

Deputy Lynn had informed Sheriff Fleming about the accident. Micah was crushed. He knew Adam and Charity well and had worked with Adam. He liked them as if they were a little sister and brother to him. Anita was brokenhearted and wanted to help.

"I'm going to the hospital to be with Charity. Micah, please tell everyone not to tell her yet about Adam's death. Wait until her mother gets here. They were so much in love. She will want to die with him. It's good she'll have the baby for comfort." Anita could hardly talk for crying.

Jacob and Jenna Mae ask an Englisch neighbor to take them to the hospital in the car. The neighbor refused pay and offered to come back for them later to go home.

Jenna Mae was crying and Jacob had moist eyes. "Ja. It is gud that Adam does not know his precious Bonnie Kate had to be put down. He is probably suffering because he can not be here with Charity and the new boppli."

"Jacob," Jenna Mae scolded, "you are so upset that you are speaking without thinking. Adam does not know. He is past feeling pain or suffering. You are forgetting *in Heaven He will wipe every tear from their eyes. There will be no more death or mourning, or crying or pain, for the old things have passed away.* (Revelation 21:4) Gott will make sure Adam has a lovely mansion of his own and will be at peace. We now need to pray for Charity to know peace and be healthy. The boppli will need her."

Deborah Yoder came to stay as long as she was needed at the Startz home. She and Matthew would be married in a month and she felt it was a duty to help Jenna Mae and take over the cooking and housework so that she could be with Charity.

Jacob had to keep working with the dairy cows and the farming. His son, Lawrence, Bradley Yoder and Kyle Snader helped with the work. The entire community was mourning the loss of Adam. They knew Charity would need a lot of moral support and help with the work on her property.

The Amish always came together to help or just be there whenever necessary.

Adam, as a good Amish, would have to be buried within three days. However the Bishop made an exception because Charity was not ready for a funeral. She had collapsed after being told of Adam's death. Trying to nurse the baby and stay calm for the new little boy's sake, she was like a zombie. She ate when made to do so and nursed the baby. That was all she could do. Her family and friends took care of everything else.

The Amish customarily wash the deceased and dress him all in white. A woman is dressed either in the clothing in which she was married or in a light colored dress with a white apron and a white kapp. There is no embalming. The Amish make a simple pine coffin with no handles or ornate markings. There is no lining. The body is simply laid in the coffin and at the grave, the coffin is placed in a plain box.

It would be longer than three days for a burial for Adam, so he was taken to a local mortician who was familiar with the Amish and their customs. His body was embalmed. He was then taken to the home for a viewing. Jacob and Jenna Mae had offered to use their home and take that much grief from Charity. She insisted that he be brought to their own home.

The furniture and everything was removed from the front room and only the coffin was there on a table. People could view the body. Friends and relatives had furnished food and woman came to help prepare and serve food. This was the first out of three viewings.

On Friday, the home was opened for a service. Pastor Chupp read Bible verses and the crowd had silent prayer. Then Bishop Eash gave a short sermon on their belief in the afterlife and how they expected to be with Jesus. He also read verses on forgiveness and spoke on not holding grudges. If they did it would be worldly and show they did not trust God to take care of the guilty.

There is no singing or eulogy. The deceased's name is spoken by the Bishop followed by prayer. Attendants file past the open casket to get a look at the deceased. Parents sometimes lift children to look. The people present are served food furnished by women of the church.

The coffin is closed and loaded on a special black wagon pulled by black horses. The black buggies line up sometimes a mile long. Police are needed to help them and keep them safe. If the Amish Cemetery is at a distance, permission is given to transport the coffin by car. Buggies still line up with family and friends.

Gravestones are commonly wood with nothing written on them. Wood is used, even though it is known it won't last long. It is to recognize the transient of time and that life is not long. The full name is never written on the marker. The church prepares what may be called a directory. It lists the name of the deceased, the cemetery where they are buried and the location of the grave in the event that someone wants to visit it later.

At the grave, there is no singing. The words of a song might be read. Bible verses are read and a prayer is given. Again the coffin is left open for any who wishes to view the body. People of the community tend to the cemetery and keep the markers as clean as possible. No flowers or any worldly items are placed on the grave.

There is no wench. Men place a rope around the coffin and lower it. The Bishop reads Bible verses or the words of a song as people walk by the grave and drop a handful of dirt on the coffin. Everyone returns to the house where women of the community feed them.

The grave is dug, and filled in, by men of the Amish community.

Weeks later Charity told friends she didn't remember details of the funeral. "I can still feel Adam's presence. He'll always be with me. He would have loved Jeremiah. He's such a happy little baby and growing so strong. Adam was looking forward to being a good Christian Amish father and teaching the Bible to our children. I know he's keeping an eye on us."

Amish practices differ from group to group, some groups the same practice Jacob was fearful that Charity would not know how to keep the property in her possession. He sent Matthew and Lawrence to stay with her for awhile and do the outside work. Matthew was preparing for his wedding and was not thinking too much about what he was doing.

In the meantime, Bishop Eash was feeling his age and not enjoying good health. He realized that he could not serve the community as he should and asked the church leaders to elect a new Bishop. The congregation would write the names of men they felt would be a good church leader. This was all done in secret. The church leaders are untrained and unpaid. It is often a burden to them. When a young man comes forward to be baptized and join the church, he is asked if he would be willing to serve the church in a leadership capacity.

The Bishop is head of the churches in the district and is responsible for the entire operation of the church. He ordains new ministers, baptizes, marries couples, conducts funerals and administers discipline to members who have broken the faith.

The ministers assist the bishop where they are needed, but the majority of their duties are to prepare and give sermons. The deacon assists the bishop, collects alms for the running of the church, publishes the couples asking for recognition and primarily carries out disciplinary issues. He is also responsible for helping members collect money and aid for medical bills they can't afford.

In Acts 1: 23-26 Paul tells how the apostles choose a new member to take the place of Judas who had betrayed Jesus and then killed himself. They voted, or cast lots, and choose Mathias. The Amish follow this method. The members submit the name of a person, in writing. It is done in secret. A minister or a deacon can be promoted if the congregation approves.

None of the men yearned for the unappreciated position of Bishop. The ministers, Joshua Chupp and Jude Nissley hoped to be left in their duties. Deacon Moses Verkler hoped he would remain in his position. He felt his family and his work took up his time and it would be difficult to fit in the duties of a Bishop.

Four names were finally chosen after many weeks of deliberations. The Bible verse of Acts 1:23-26 was written on a slip of paper. Four song books were selected and the verse was placed in one of them. The books were shifted around making it impossible to know which book the slip of paper was in.

After the long Sunday service, four men were called to come to the front. Jacob Startz, Moses Yoder, Amos Snader and Joseph Lehman reluctantly walked slowly to the front. They were told to each pick up a song book. Moses Yoder had the book with the verse in it. The other men breathed a sigh of relief. A time would be set later for the ordination and a celebration dinner.

CHAPTER THIRTEEN

Charity was thankful that Adam had taught her how to work with his wood cutting tools which left her with one possibility of earning money to support herself and little Jeremiah. She refused financial assistance from Jacob or Joshua Kime. The two men got together and purchased a building for a store that was being sold not far from Charity's home.

Jenna Mae helped clean the building and the men put in shelves. Bishop Yoder gave permission for electrical lines to be run into the store to run a freezer, a refrigerator and ceiling fans. They knew Charity would be taking the baby to work with her. She could also use heating fans. He agreed to the contact with worldly appliances because he knew Charity was a good, honest Amish woman and would not be influenced.

Neighbors donated meat for the freezer to be sold. Others made arrangements to barter eggs, butter and milk for items for sewing. Charity had work Adam had completed in addition to her own as well as honey and flowers. She could sell vegetables in season. She agreed to offer the beautiful hand made quilts for sale for a small fee. This was one way the Amish worked together. Everyone wanted her to have an income without her feeling as if she was accepting charity.

Charity was not enthused with the idea at first and was reluctant to even go look at the store, but Jacob convinced her to consider it for her baby's sake. He reminded her that Jeremiah would need many things that they did not grow and he would be growing and need more. Jenna Mae told her how proud Adam would be of her for being independent. She finally acquiesced.

Alicia and Maeve were delighted and determined to help her when they were not in school. Belinda and Marysue Kime wanted to be included because they were Adam's little sisters which made them Jeremiah's aunts. Their arguments were so sound that Charity smiled at their tenacity.

Jacob and Joshua would always be available. Quinn Kime, Kyle Snader and Michael Lehman privately made a pact to be of assistance. Nadine suggested that Charity put in a stove with a good oven to sell some of her delicious pies, cakes and other items. She even begged Charity to allow her to work with her when she could.

October came roaring in with a cold wind and icy rain. Matthew and Deborah were making final plans for their wedding. Charity wanted it to be a memorable occasion for them as it was for her. She smiled to herself thinking of what a shaky start she and Adam had to their marriage and how much in love they were very soon after the wedding.

Oliver Snader informed them that he had enough of rumspringa. He was ready to be a real Amish man and be baptized. He would be eighteen in December. Bishop Yoder and Deacon Verkler talked to him impressing him with all he would need to learn and remember.

Their sessions included the original plans from 1632 and what they followed now. They warned him about dating or falling for a girl who was not of their faith and had not been baptized in the church.

2 Corinthians 6:14 *Do not be equally yoked with unbelievers for what do righteousness and wickedness have in common?*

2 Corinthians 6:17 *Therefore come away from them and be separate.*

Romans 12:2 *Do not conform any longer to the pattern of this world, but be transformed by the renewing of your mind. Then you will be able to test and approve what God's will is.*

Hebrews 13:5 *Keep your lives free from the love of money and be content with what you have for God has said, "Never will I leave you; never will I forsake you."*

1 Peter 5:76-9 *Cast all your anxiety on Him because He cares for you. Be self-controlled and alert. Your enemy, the devil, prowls around like a roaring lion. Resist him, standing firm in the faith, because you know your brothers throughout the world are undergoing the same kind of sufferings.*

There were many more verses to help church members know why they practice the faith that they do and how they must follow God's teachings. Oliver had no idea there would be nine sessions and teaching from the church leaders, but he willing listened and learned. He learned that Anabaptist meant re-baptized. The Amish, Mennonites and Quakers believe that a person should not be baptized until they can learn Bible teachings, know what it means in their lives and can promise to follow the teachings. He was pleased that three of his male friends and two female friends were going through with him.

Two worship services prior to the autumn communion, the young people were taken out of the service and given a chance to talk to a minister and change their minds about being baptized and thus a member of the church. They all wanted to continue.

During a special service there were hymns, Bible verses and sermons. Finally the young people were called to the front to kneel in front of the church leaders and the congregation.

The Bishop asked the congregation if they were willing to accept these young people and would promise to help them stand firm in the faith. There were loud choruses of "JA" all over the room.

The girls' white prayer kapp was removed leaving them bareheaded. Deacon Verkler stepped forward holding a wooden bucket of water and a tin cup. The Bishop cupped his hands and held the water. Three times for each person he would say, "I baptize you in the name of the Father, (water) the Son (water) and the Holy Ghost (water)," as he sprinkled the water three times on each head.

As he finished he asked them to stand and said, "Upon your faith which you have confessed before God and these many witnesses, you are baptized. In the name of the Lord and the church, we extend to you the hand of fellowship. Rise and be a faithful member of the church." Bishop would then give the Holy Kiss (a kiss on both cheeks) to each young man, but the Deacon's wife would give the Holy Kiss to the girls.

There was much rejoicing and a big feast to follow. This was a solemn and joyous occasion as were the marriage vows.

Charity was doing well in the store. She insisted on paying rent to Jacob and Joshua even though they didn't want it. Rosemary had married also in October and was gladly coming on some days to be with Nadine and Charity. They were thankful and pleased with friendship shown upon them by Anita Fleming, Catherine Alicea, Victoria Bolling and the Barrington family as well as auslander friends these ladies brought in.

Charity happily built birdhouses, doghouses and other wooden items that were sold as quickly as she could make them. Also her bakery products became known all over the country and people were coming from a distance to trade with her.

Her brother, Lawrence, and Kyle Snader, worked one full day to work the dirt around the building and plant beautiful, colorful flowers and flowering shrubbery. In the spring they would dig up a section of ground behind the store to grow a few vegetables and herbs.

A covered porch ran around two sides of the building which gave shelter for customers and a place for Charity and her friends to rock and talk when they found the time.

Charity would have been very happy if she could get over the way Adam was killed. She was distressed that no one had found who was driving the car that hit them. Her faith demanded that she not feel hate or any ugly feeling toward the person who had killed her beloved Adam. She struggled with this, but did pray a lot and asked God to give her the strength to forget and to be a good mother to her precious little boy. This was the only time that she, for a short time, regretted not having pictures of Adam or mementoes to share with Jermiah when he was old enough to appreciate them. She considered having a portrait painted which was allowed.

She carried the baby in a cloth sling across her chest often. Other times she made a bed for him on quilts and pads behind the counter in the store. She wanted the baby to know he was loved and wanted.

Thanksgiving was a hollow day for Charity. She ate with her parents and friends who had been invited to join them. She smiled when they passed her baby around and cooed at him how beautiful he was. Alicia and Maeve went home with her for a few days to help her with the housework and give her some company.

Nadine, Deborah and Rosemary could be found at the store with Charity often. They were delighted to help keep the store clean and wait on customers. Rosemary was looking forward to being a mother.

December came lumbering in with snow and cold, strong winds. Charity was thankful for the heat in her store for the baby's sake, although she continued to believe Amish about not having worldly things about them. She was not tempted to indulge in worldly helps.

The boys brought her vines, mistletoe and items to make into wreaths. Charity and the girls made many beautiful wreaths for Christmas out of berries, vines and items of nature. They sold well in the store.

Amish exchange gifts but do not celebrate Christmas except for the ministers to tell the meaning of Christmas and the birth of Jesus.

Adam's mother had dressed in nothing but black for a year following his death. Charity wore the black dress and made some black aprons. She already had black hose, shoes and bonnets. After the first of the year she began wearing grey aprons she made while in the store.

The Amish never talked of Adam's death, but Charity's Englisch friends would ask if there was any news about who was driving the car. Charity would shake her head, but wouldn't talk about it.

One day Anita Fleming was in the store when some women she knew came in and asked about the driver. "I feel that God will work on the driver and force a confession. Remember how the young people agonized over the cruel behavior over those who were harassing the nice people? They finally came forward and told what they knew. Micah put all the conversations together and found the guilty ones. I'm confident that God will allow that to happen in this case."

The ladies were impressed and there was a lot of chit-chat about it. More talking in the neighborhood, in church and in groups. One day Lisa Kennedy was with a social group who began to discuss the criminal who ran the buggy off the road, killed the horse and almost killed the family which included three little children.

"I was so shocked when I heard of it. That must be a monstrous person who would deliberately run into them and then drive on and say nothing. We were so upset when our son died and we were angry at everyone, including the innocent Amish. I was pleased to hear later they had nothing to do with my son's death, but my husband is still heartbroken. He knows Darren killed himself, but he still declares if the Amish had not been living here, it never would have happened."

The talk gradually changed to plans for raising money for a new gazebo in the city park and a better playground for the children.

Later the same evening Lisa thought of the conversation she had with the ladies and decided to discuss it with her husband, Dr. Willfred Kennedy, when he returned from his lodge meeting. He came through the door throwing his coat over a chair in the living room and settling down with a grunt in his lounge chair.

"Willfred, I've been thinking about something."

"Well, hooray. Did you notify the president and take an ad in the paper?"

"Goodness, what's got you so riled? You don't need to be so ugly with me. I don't know --"

"That's it. You don't know. You don't know about anything, but you can sure run your mouth about everything you know nothing about."

She realized he had been drinking. "What are you talking about? I don't know how to approach you any more. It doesn't matter what the subject is, you blame me for your bad feelings and take all your frustrations out on me. Darren is my son, too. We should have been comforting each other, but instead you took off in a direction that I can't understand. I can't seem to talk to you about anything without you getting angry with me. I wish you'd tell me if something is wrong with you. Are you worried about the business? What is it?"

He jumped up to run right in her face; so close she drew back thinking he acted as if he might hit her. He just scowled at her, grabbed his coat on and ran out again.

"Willfred, don't drive. Please don't go out again. You're in no condition to be driving. What if you have an accident?"

He stopped on the porch looking back with an indescribable grin on his face. "I've had accidents before and I'm doing fine." he laughed manically and stumbled to his car.

Lisa wondered why he had left his car out instead of driving into the garage. She showered and prepared for bed. Drinking hot chocolate she waited for him to come home. Waking up with a sore neck and back, she realized she had gone to sleep on the couch with the lights on. It was beginning to be daylight. Had Willfred come home and gone on to bed?

No. He wasn't in bed and no sign of him in the house. His car was still gone. Should she call the police and ask if an accident had been reported or should she check with the hospital? Heartsick and worried, she made a pot of coffee and planned a wonderful breakfast when he did come home.

Noon came and went and still no word from her husband. Even though she knew he didn't like her and they had never been friendly, she called his brother, Orville Kennedy, in Wilkes Barre. Willfred and Orville were very close and often got together.

"Hello." A woman's voice answered.

"Jasmine?"

"Yes."

"This is Lisa. Have you heard from Willfred recently?"

"Let me let you talk to Orville."

There was a silence and a short wait. The phone clunked against something as it was picked up. "Yeah?" A man's angry voice answered.

"Orville?"

"You called me. Whatdaya want?"

"I hate to bother you, but ___"

"Well, why do you?"

"Do I what?"

"Bother me, stupid. Why did you call me?"

"Forgive me, but I wanted to know if you had talked, or heard, from Willfred recently."

"Yeah. What's it to you?"

"I AM his wife and I'm concerned about him. He was drinking when he left here last night and hasn't returned. I'm worried."

A sarcastic laugh came over the phone. "If you hadn't run him off, you'd know where he is."

"I. Did. Not. Run him off. I take it he's there and has told you something that is untrue. I want to speak to him."

"Now you want to speak to him." Another crazy laugh. "I'll ask him if he wants to speak to you. I can't make him." The phone dropped with a bang.

"Yeah. What do you want?"

"Willfred. I've been so worried about you. Why did you leave as you did and why didn't you return home?"

"We'll talk about this when I get home."

"When are you coming home?"

"Look for me when you see me coming." There was a lot of loud laughter as he hung up.

Lisa collapsed in tears and began to pray wondering what she should do.

CHAPTER FOURTEEN

Charity was so thankful for her family, friends and church family. The loss of Adam would never be easy, but she was beginning to adjust. She prayed a lot and read the big family Bible aloud to Jeremiah just as Adam had looked forward to doing. He was too young to understand, but he would grow up knowing that the Bible must be read and learned and prayers said.

Jeremiah was a happy, healthy baby and smiled at everyone who looked at him. Everyone, who came into the store, made over the baby. Her Englisch friends offered to baby sit if she needed them, but she knew her family and church friends were available. She thanked them and said nothing.

Matthew had carried the swinging cradle that Adam had made to the store. Jeremiah was gurgling happily in the cradle one day when auslander tourists came in. They exclaimed over the clean store and all that was for sale. Charity realized they didn't mean to be rude, but they did ask questions about how she and the girls were dressed and about their faith. One of the men said he was a youth minister in a church in Wilkes Barre and was interested in knowing more about the Amish.

Rosemary shyly told him that he should talk to the church leaders and not to the women. He asked why. She stated that even though they knew about the church and their faith that it was the duty of the men to tell about them.

He didn't understand why the women couldn't tell him, but his wife touched his arm and said, "Be respectful of their beliefs. Maybe they're not permitted to talk, especially to men that are not of their faith."

Charity, Rosemary and Maeve just smiled at them. At that moment Jeremiah gave a cry of pain. Charity rushed to his side with everyone following her.

One of the women stepped in. "Forgive me, but I'm a pediatrician-- baby doctor, and I'd like to help."

Charity was so concerned about her baby that she spoke mostly in her language. Of course the woman could not understand, but did understand that she was a distressed mother.

"Please, let me hold the little one and check him. It may be nothing, then again he may need medical help."

Charity reluctantly held her baby over to the woman doctor and said a silent prayer. Looking toward Rosemary and Maeve she knew they were praying, too.

"My name is Bonnie Kate Mercer. This is my husband, Bernard. These are friends of ours Bill and Emily Hutchinson.

Charity paled at the name of Bonnie Kate, bit her lower lip and kept silent. Bonnie pulled the covers off Jeremiah and admired the sweet white gown with embroidery on it. She knew Charity had made it.

"Oh, my. There's a bite of some kind on his arm. It looks as if it might be a spider."

With that Charity gave a cry and reached for her baby. "No, please let me see what I can do. Has he ever shown signs of being allergic to anything?"

"No. He's a very healthy baby," Rosemary answered. She saw that Charity was too overcome to talk.

"I'm sorry I don't have anything with me to treat him. Let's get him to a hospital and they will have everything we need."

"I'll go get Kyle to bring a buggy," Maeve started to run out the door.

"We'll take my car. It's quicker," Bill Hutchinson said.

Rosemary urged Charity to go and take the baby. She and Maeve would take care of the store. Charity hugged her precious baby close to her heart and got in the car. In a matter of minutes they were at Mercy Hospital.

Bonnie Kate placed a firm, loving arm around Charity and hurried her and the baby into the Emergency Room.

"I'm Dr. Bonnie Mercer and I need to see a doctor immediately."

Two nurses scurried out to find someone while one called over the speaker phone. "Dr. Grover, you're wanted immediately in the E R. Dr. Grover, please come to the E R immediately." Another nurse took them quickly into a cubicle. She had no more than pulled the curtain around the opening when a man came rushing in looking tired and worried.

"I'm Dr. Grover. What's the problem?" His wheat colored hair looked as if he had been in a wind storm and his kind blue eyes took in the group at once. He immediately reached for the baby and placed him on a padded table.

"I'm Dr. Mercer, but I'm not from here. The baby seems to have a spider bite on his left arm. I didn't know whether it was poison or not."

"Let me see. It isn't showing signs of being a poisonous bite, but it was wise of you to bring him in." He turned looking a little surprised to see Charity. "Hello. Is this your baby?"

"Ja. I mean yes, it is. He's all I have and I don't want anything to happen to him."

"Well, we're going to make sure he's A-okay hunky-dory," he smiled. "Do I know you? You look familiar."

"I don't know. You could have seen me in here when my baby was born."

"What's your name?"

"Charity Startz Kime. This is Jeremiah."

He thought a moment. "Oh, yes. I remember now. You were brought in following a buggy accident and had your baby almost before you could get here. I don't remember all the circumstances. There are hundreds of people who come through here, but some make an impression on me. I remember you and your family because of your faith that God would take care of everything. I believe, also, even though we are not of the same faith."

Charity tried to smile but didn't feel like it. "My husband was killed in the accident the same day my baby was born. He never got to see his son and he had been so happy planning for a child." She stifled a sob.

"Oh, yes. I'm so sorry I brought it up. "He asked a nurse to bring an injection of one tenth CC of corticosteroid. Turning to Dr. Mercer he explained. "I don't think it is a poison bite and can't even be sure it was a spider, but I'm following what I know to do." He then spoke to Charity.

"Mrs. Kime. I'm washing the bite well with soap and water and drying thoroughly. I'll give the injection and then place a cold pack on his arm. I think he's too young for acetaminophen, but I will give you an antibiotic cream to rub on the spot. If there is any redness, swelling or he gets real cranky, bring him back to me. I do honestly think this will take care of it."

Jeremiah gave a scream of protest when the tiny needle pricked his arm. He quietened when his mother cuddled him and crooned to him.

Bonnie Kate hugged Charity. "I'm glad we were able to help you and am so relieved that it isn't something worse. He's a beautiful baby and is so happy. I can tell you love each other. I'm sorry. I couldn't help but hear what you told Dr. Grover. You've had too much sorrow in your young life. You're so brave to have your work to support you and your baby. I'm sure you have family and friends willing to help."

"Ja. Danki" She blushed. "Yes, thank you. I'm very grateful to you for getting us here so quickly. I need to pay before we can leave."

Bernard and Bill were standing near. "You don't owe anything," Bill said. "That's all been taken care of."

Charity was embarrassed. "Oh, I can pay. I don't need someone else to pay my bills."

"It wasn't much and we're glad to help," Emily hugged Charity. "I just want you to know I'm humbled to meet you and will come again to trade with you."

"Let's get you back or your friends will be worried," Bonnie said laughing as she ushered the group out to the car.

"At least let me pay you for bringing me," Charity begged.

"Nope. Nada. Nix. Nill," Bernard laughed. "It is our pleasure and we count it as a blessing for us. You see, we believe in God and in sharing with anyone who needs us, just as you do."

Deacon Verkler was coming out of the store when the car stopped and they all got out. He looked at Charity and she was fearful he would scold her. He came to them and looked smiling down at Jeremiah. "I hear what happened. It is Gottes wille these nice people were here. Danki. Got segen eich." He walked on over to his buggy.

"What did he say?" Bernard whispered to Charity.

Her laughter bubbled out loud. "He said thank you and God bless you."

Bill frowned. "But he said something else at first."

Charity thought. "Oh. He said it was God's will for you to be here. Please come in. I want to give you something."

Bonnie backed away. "We don't need anything. We do feel blessed that we got to meet you and were here to help you."

"Please kumme. I have my own bee hives and we have good clover honey with the comb in it. I want to share with you."

"I guess kumme means come," Bonnie laughed. "Okay. This one time. We will be back though and trade with you. I want to see this beautiful, bouncing baby boy. He'll grow too fast. You'll wish he would stay a baby longer."

Rosemary and Maeve were anxiously waiting to hear about Jeremiah.

They were so grateful to the auslanders. Maeve ran to get two pint jars of the honey for Charity. She also included two loaves of Friendship bread.

Before they left Charity hugged the women. She turned to Bonnie with sad eyes. "I'm sorry if you wondered about me when you told us you name. My husband's favorite horse was named Bonnie Kate and she was killed with the buggy accident. He never knew that either or it would have broken his heart."

"I don't know what to say. The more I talk to you the more I admire you. To be so young and have to shoulder so many heartaches." she sighed. "We need to count our blessings more and be more aware of those around us."

They told the three young women bye. Before they left Bernard did something to Jeremiah's little blanket. After they left Maeve went over out of curiosity to see what he did. There was a note wrapped around two twenty dollar bills and a ten dollar bill. "Keep this for your precious little boy. I hope it can be a start to help him with his dreams some day."

Charity didn't know what to do. "I told them we did not take charity. Why did he do this?"

Rosemary patted her back. "I don't think they look at it as charity. They like you and want to be good Christians, so they want to leave something that Jeremiah can use when he gets bigger."

"I'll give it back to them when they come back. They said they would come back."

Maeve protested. "I don't think that would be kind. They said it was a blessing to them to meet you. Ask your daed what you should do."

Charity nodded. "Ja. Ask daed."

The three girls looked startled when someone came running in the door breathing heavily. Lisa Kennedy's eyes were wild looking and she was in distress.

"Oh, my dear. I'm so, so sorry. I don't know what to do."

Rosemary placed a hand on her arm. "What is troubling you? How can we help?"

She started sobbing. "I don't know what I'm doing here. You can't help. But I do need help. I need to talk to someone."

Charity patted Lisa's back. "If we can't help, maybe you should talk to your pastor, Rev. Barrington."

"That's it. That's who I'll talk to. He can't tell what I say unless I give him permission, can he? Thank you. I'm so sorry. I'll go talk to him. He's probably in his office at the church."

She ran out in a flurry leaving the girls stunned.

"Wonder what that was all about?" Maeve questioned.

"Don't have an idea," Rosemary sniffed.

"It is none of our business," Charity reminded them. "Rev. Barrington is the one she needs to tell about her troubles. Poor lady. We need to pray for her."

Charity went back to taking care of her baby. Rosemary continued dusting and cleaning. Maeve continued straighten items and sweeping the floor.

CHAPTER FIFTEEN

Charity went home that night happy to cuddle her baby and talk to him. He was now almost six months old and was sitting up. He babbled lovingly at one and all and loved life. He loved the animals and reached for the kittens and dogs as if they were stuffed toys. They soon learned to dodge the baby.

He kicked and laughed gleefully when his uncle Matthew put him on a horse in front of him and went for a ride. Jeremiah would look at everything and point excitedly and babble as if he were trying to tell Matthew what he was seeing.

A few days passed and Charity forgot about Lisa Kennedy. The Sunday service was at the Kime residence. Charity gladly went over to help her in-laws prepare for the wonderful day. There were many hands to play with Jeremiah and keep him giggling while his mother cleaned and sewed. She baked and cooked in preparation for the dinner.

The Sunday service was well attended. They people were not only glad to worship, but this gave them a chance to eat together and socialize. They all worked so hard it was difficult to do much else.

Joseph Lehman, the song leader had led in two very long songs. Bishop Moses Yoder had read several scriptures. Ministers Joshua Chupp and Jude Nissley were ready to preach when the door burst open and a woman ran in. Her long, black hair needed combing. It was standing all around her head like several angry snakes. Her amber eyes were flashing wildly. She was in a long, pink silk nightgown and barefoot.

The woman didn't look as if she were focusing her eyes. She began to moan and cry. "I'm so sorry. I didn't kill anybody, but I know who did. I'm so sorry, so sorry, so sorry." She kept yelling. She ran about half way down the aisle and began to pitch forward in a faint. Cathrine Yoder and Jenna Mae Startz were sitting on the end of a bench near her and both jumped up to catch her.

Bishop Yoder asked for everyone to stay seated and as quiet as possible. "Does anyone know who this woman is?"

Charity stood. "Ja. Her name is Mrs. Kennedy. Her husband is a dentist in town."

"Poor soul," Nadine Lapp said. "She seems to have had a mind breakdown."

"What must we do?" Several voices spoke.

Jacob Startz came and picked her up. "Wife, let us go to the kitchen. Lawrence, go to the Morrison home, or any Englischer that has a phone, and call for Micah. He will know what to do. She needs a doctor."

Jacob, Jenna Mae and Deborah hurried to the kitchen with the woman. Bishop Yoder was torn. He felt he should go to see about the woman and he should stay and continue the service. But if the service continued, they would be interrupted again when help came for the woman. He looked at his son-in-law, Matthew Startz.

"Matthew, please wait outside and bring Micah through the side door into the kitchen. We will go on with our worship."

The Amish were still human and curious about the woman, but they followed the suggestion of their Bishop and continued with the service. The younger people were restless and curious. They had more than one adult glare at them and shake a head for their looking around and whispering.

There was a short pause in Minister Jude Nissley's sermon when a siren was heard drawing near. They could hear voices from the other side of the house. Jude cleared his throat and talked on. When even the adults began to feel restless, Joseph Lehman stood and led in a song. This was followed by a silent prayer. Bishop cleared his throat to alert them that the prayer was completed.

The women hurried into the kitchen to get the food ready and to find out what was going on. The men gathered on the front lawn where they could talk and see around the building. The young people hurried out in hopes of satisfying their curiosity.

Micah was waiting and saw that the service was over. He came forward and asked Bishop Yoder if he could talk to the people. He was given permission. Everyone came back inside where they could hear.

Micah was well known and well liked. He first thanked everyone for their patience and cooperation and then apologized for the disturbance.

"I don't know yet why Mrs. Kennedy was here, especially in the condition she is in. She has not been able to talk to us and tell us why she is so upset. Doctor Marcus Ford was called in to be with her and we have gotten in touch with her husband. I also called her minister and advised him of the situation. I can only thank you again for your valuable help and cooperation. It might be several days before we know the entire truth of whatever is going on. I'll tell your Bishop as soon as I known what to say and he can inform the rest of you. I'm sorry your service was interrupted. God bless you all."

Willfred Kennedy, his brother Orville and Orvile's oldest son, Porter had been on a trip somewhere. Lisa had been in the hospital for three days, but was still unconscious. Willfred was more upset at what she might have said rather than the condition she was in.

"What has she told you? None of you can pay any attention to her. She's crazy. I bet she was drunk."

"Oh, no," Dr. Ford answered angrily. "She had not even been drinking. My opinion is that she has been so upset with something she knows. She was thinking so strongly about it that she temporarily lost her reasoning ability. She's under stress. She'll be fine after she rests for a few days."

"Well, when she comes to, call me," Willfred demanded. "I don't want anyone else talking to her." He stomped out of the hospital.

"Humph! Can you imagine? I've known some hard-hearted people in my twenty-eight years of nursing, but I've never met one so uncaring about his own wife." Nurse Carrie Fuller shook her head and went about her duties.

"What do we do now?" Nurse Doris Young asked. "I've only worked a year, but I'm appalled at his behavior. Do we notify him before the Sheriff? After all Sheriff Fleming did ask to be notified as soon as she was able to talk."

Doctor Ford admonished all listening to not talk about this to anyone else and to call him as soon as she showed signs of rousing. He went into his office, bowed his head and prayed. He then picked up the phone and called Micah.

"Sheriff, I might be accused of being unprofessional, however, I don't feel right about this. My patient comes first-- always. Mrs. Kennedy was afraid as well as upset over something when she came in. I will call you as soon as she's able to talk, but ethically I have to call her husband, also."

"I understand, Dr. Ford and I appreciate the position it puts you in. May I ask that you call me a few minutes before you call Dr. Kennedy?"

He sighed deeply. "Yes, I'll do that, and I'll write on her chart that no one is to talk to anyone about her condition until I've had a chance to examine her."

"Thank you. I'll be waiting for your call." the two men hung up their phones. They would have smiled if they had known that both of them said a prayer before leaving their desks.

The following Sunday was not a worship day. The Amish did no work, but visited each other and rested. Jacob was outside the barn talking to two neighbor men when a car roared in spewing gravels and tearing up grass.

"Was est letz do mit demmkopp? (What is wrong with this dummy?)" Joseph Lehman sputtered.

"He est ob im kopp, (He is off in the head)" Benjamin Lapp answered.

Jacob just stood straight and looked at the car as the driver got out. Another man got out of the passenger side. The driver was slightly staggering.

"What fool owns this property? Is this where Jacob Startz lives? What a crazy name."

"Of course it's crazy. They're Aim-esh, ain't they?" The second man laughed uproariously.

The first man drew himself up as if he were going to make an important speech. "I'm Doctor Kennedy, and I want you to take a message to all your crazy Aim-esh people. Keep your noses out of my business and leave my wife alone or there'll be trouble."

Jacob spoke soothingly. "We do not tend to other people's business and we have not bothered your wife. We did not even know who she was when she came into our worship service last Sunday. Please leave and don't bother us."

Willfred walked toward Jacob in a threatening gesture. At that moment a car pulled up with two deputies in it. Deputies Roy Braun and Harlan Moelus got out in a hurry. "Good. We're just in time. We've been following this speed demon and trying to stop him before he caused a serious accident. You two men are under arrest."

They walked toward Willfred and his brother, Orville. They knew there would be a confrontation.

Orville drunkenly squared off for battle. "Get away from me or I'll put you in the ground. I know kick boxing." He raised a leg and kicked out losing his balance and throwing himself on the ground. Roy quickly snapped cuffs on him. Harlan had no trouble cuffing Willfred.

The two prisoners were put in the back seat of the police car where a metal petition was between then and the front seat. Harlan drove them to the county jail while Roy drove their car to park it in the impound lot.

Micah drove in about a half hour later to apologize for the men getting as far as they did. "My men had no idea where they were headed. They only knew the car was being driven too fast and often swinging all over the road."

Jacob assured him there were no hard feelings. "I don't know why they came here. I've had nothing to do with any of them."

"Jacob, it's impossible to know what a drunk is thinking. Let me know if any of them give you more trouble." He left and Jacob went into the house to discuss it with Jenna Mae. He knew she had observed it through the window and would be curious.

The following Wednesday, ten days after Lisa Kennedy's breakdown, Micah got a call from Dr. Ford. "Mrs. Kennedy is awake and slightly confused. I'll wait a few minutes and call her husband."

Micah rushed over to the hospital and up to Lisa's room. He eased into the room and stood where Lisa could see him, but he would not appear threatening. "Hello, Mrs. Kennedy. I'm glad to see you're awake. You had me worried."

She replied weakly. "I understand I'm in the hospital and have been here for several days. Do you know why I'm here?"

"I only know you were very sick and passed out. You seemed to be worried about something and felt you needed to tell someone about it. Will I do? I'll be happy to listen to you."

"I don't know," she said rubbing her temples with her finger tips. "I just can't think. Maybe you can help me."

He didn't want to rush her or put pressure on her that would cause a further breakdown. "Let's just take it easy and talk. Maybe it will come back to you."

She relaxed and was just starting to say something when her door was pushed open. Willfred charged in staring angrily at Micah. "What are you doing here? What has she said to you? Pay no attention to what ever she might say. She's a drunk and has trouble with her thoughts."

Lisa began to cry. "How can you talk to me that way? You claim to love me. We have three children, or rather had three. Your temper and sinful example caused the death of our oldest, our only son. Now you pay no attention to your daughters or to me. You just run to Orville all the time. What are the two of you hiding? What are you guilty of?"

She was exhausted and fell back on the pillow looking pale and weak. Micah hurriedly pushed the button calling for a nurse. Carrie Fuller came rushing in taking charge of the situation. "Out! Out! Both of you. My patient needs her rest." She was not intimidated by Willfred.

"She's my wife and I have a right to be here," he sputtered belligerently.

"I don't care if you're the President of the United States. You're not going to stay in this room and upset my patient." Micah left walking in such a way that Willfred had to leave ahead of him or get walked on.

Willfred sputtered, cursed and fumed all the way down the hall. "I'll have the law on you." He yelled at Micah. "No one treats me this way."

Micah could hardly keep from laughing, but he knew it would just make Willfred more angry. Calmly he stated, "I **am** the law. We are both leaving and let the doctors and nurses work with your wife to make her better."

"Nothing is going to make her better. She imagines a lot of crazy things. I need to talk to her."

"You can do that when she is well enough to talk. At the present time she needs rest and free from stress."

Grumbling, Willfred did leave looking back to glare at Micah. He said something to some nurses as he passed them that caused them to gasp and looked alarmed after him. Micah thought it best if he left, also. He couldn't keep from thinking.

What was on Mrs. Kennedy's mind that was so shattering? Did she know something about a death or someone breaking the law? Did she know something that would put Willfred in prison? Is that what worried Willfred? He hoped to get the answers soon.

CHAPTER SIXTEEN

Two days later Micah was in Lisa's room as soon as he was allowed in. He hoped to be in and out before Mr. Kennedy showed up. He was not surprised when the nurses told him Mr. Kennedy had not been back and Mrs. Kennedy seemed relieved.

He quietly walked beside her bed trying not to disturb her, but she opened her eyes and looked at him. He was pleased to see her eyes were more alert and she showed signs of being able to think and talk.

"Good morning," he smiled. "How are you feeling now?"

"Good morning. I feel fine, much better than I've been feeling. Is Willfred anywhere around?"

"No. I'm sorry. Did you want me to get him?"

"NO. Oh, sorry. I need to talk to you privately." He sat in the chair by her bedside and waited. "I don't know how to start."

"Start anywhere you please. I'm not here to judge you, just to listen."

"To begin I don't have any proof of what I'm going to tell you. I only know about the expressions I've seen on my husband's face, about his reactions to certain subjects and change in personality. His dental practice has suffered and he is not the same man I married. I don't know whether it's because of Darren's death or if he's involved as I suspect him to be."

Micah sat quietly with no expression. He knew from experience that most people could not stand silence. If he kept quiet they would talk about anything they thought of and sometimes it was just what he wanted to know.

She continued. "Well, after that nice Mr. Kime was killed, Willfred seemed to have something on his mind. He wouldn't talk to me, but he did get with his brother, Orville, a lot. They're only fourteen months apart and are very close. As time passed, he got worse. He drinks more, he neglects his work, he runs to his brother's and he is angry with me over nothing and everything. I can't say or do anything that he approves of."

She pinched the sheet between her fingers and nervously glanced at Micah out of the corner of her eye. "I asked him point blank one day if he was guilty of something and he threw a fit, storming out and driving to his brother's to be gone a couple of days. At first I didn't know where he was. I don't know what he told them, but Orville and his wife have been ugly to me. I stopped trying to talk to either of them until the Sunday morning I lost control and went looking for someone to listen to me. I'm so ashamed that I interrupted the worship service, but there is where I began to get some help. Did you know several of the Amish have visited me and are concerned? I don't understand how anyone can hate them so much when they are so kind."

Micah shifted on the hard seat. He was trying desperately to remain calm and quiet to encourage her to feel free to talk.

"As I said I don't have definite proof. That Sunday Willfred apparently thought I was still asleep. He was on the phone with his brother. I heard him say, 'Don't be worried. I'll keep it to myself and Lisa doesn't have to know. She would just blab it all over the county. I don't care what you've done, I'll stand by you no matter what. The more Amish we can get rid of, the better off we'll be.'"

"He looked up then and saw me looking at him. He screamed at me and hung the phone up, yelling at me that if I said one word of what I had heard to anybody that I would join that Amish man in his grave. I lost it.

He ran out of the house and I guess I lost control and went hunting someone I could talk to. I'm so very sorry that I upset the Amish in their service."

"They do not hold that against you. In fact they've been praying for you and want to help if they can. Remember they do not hate or hold grudges."

Micah leaned forward and took her hand. "Do you think Willfred was the one driving the car that killed Adam Kime?"

"I did at first, but now I think his brother is guilty and he's helping cover up for his brother. What can I do? What can you do?" She clung to his hand.

"I can't do anything because, as you said, there is no proof. Our only chance is to somehow trick him into saying enough that I have grounds to arrest him and question him. A slick attorney would make mince meat of us and we'd lose a chance of finding the guilty party. Do me a favor. Keep quiet. Say absolutely nothing to Willfred about any of this. Play dumb. Let him get careless thinking you know nothing and haven't told me anything."

Micah realized that Lisa was now afraid of Willfred and his brother. She needed to be home with her youngest daughter who was a junior in high school. The older girl was away at college. They talked a few minutes more and he reminded her to pretend that all was well between her and Willfred.

As Micah started out the hospital door, he saw Willfred walking in from the parking lot. He quickly backed up and looked around for somewhere to stand so that he would not be noticed. He saw a restroom sign pointing around a corner and headed that way. He waited a few minutes and came out to walk to the parking lot hoping Willfred would not know he had been there.

For some reason, she could not explain, Charity felt compelled to visit Mrs. Kennedy a few times. They always talked about Jeremiah and the store. Charity was in the room one afternoon when Mr. Kennedy came in. Cold chills ran up her spine at the expression in his eyes when he discovered her. She quickly told Lisa and Willfred that she was praying for them and hurried out.

Jeremiah was proudly standing now by holding to furniture or people's legs. He was very independent and wanted to do things on his own.

Jacob laughed and said, "That rascal is going to be running before long. Just wait until you have to go through rumspringa with him, then you'll know what it is to be anxious. We never had worries with you, dochder.

You were not interested in rumspringa except for a few weeks." He paused. "I need to wash the outside of your store. There is a weschp (wasp) building a nest near the front corner. You don't want anyone stung."

Jacob left the store as Amish friends came in. They wished each other a gut daag (good day) and talked of the usual things of interest to them.

The woman left the men talking while she went in to buy some brawn shugah (brown sugar). She also bought a large wooden schpoon (spoon) for stirring jams and jellies she was making.

Charity thankfully closed for the day and bid her helpers a fond good bye as she locked the door behind her. Lawrence was waiting with a buggy to take her and Jeremiah home.

Micah made excuses to talk to Willfred Kennedy about Lisa's hospital stay. "Mr. Kennedy, is there anything I can do to help? Do you have any idea why your wife is so stressed out?" He leaned against his car.

"No, and it's nobody's business but ours. She isn't right in the head for some reason. Maybe she's been sick or taking medicine that I don't know about. Has she said anything to you?"

"Such as? I don't know what you mean. What would she talk to me about?"

"I don't know. She's crazy."

"She's been upset every since your son died. It was a big enough shock to know of his death and then to find that he killed himself."

"No. He didn't set out to kill himself."

"I know that, Mr. Kennedy. Get a group of kids together, especially boys, and they will try to show off for each other. I'm sure he had no idea he would die."

"He'd still be alive if those blamed Amish did not live so close."

"What do the Amish have to do with it?"

"Well, none of the decent people want them here. They are a drain on our economy and do nothing to help."

"I'm sorry you feel that way, Mr. Kennedy. They are not a drain on the economy. They pay taxes, they trade in our stores, they furnish food for our tables and milk. They are good workers and stay to themselves. They are strictly against quarreling or fighting of any kind. They believe in live and let live. They would never think of doing something bad to you or your property.'"

"Just the fact that they're here is bad enough."

"Have any of them done anything to you to cause you to feel this way? How does your brother feel about them?"

"They've done nothing personally to me. Just being here is annoying with their strange clothing and them going around like zombies. My brother hates them more than I do."

Micah hoped he would continue talking without realizing that his brother had been brought into the conversation. "Has your brother had some problems with the Amish?"

Willfred laughed manically. "Problems with them. No, but they've sure had some with him."

"Really? How's that?"

Willfred slowly swung his head like a bull that didn't know whether to charge or not. "I've said too much. Has my crazy wife said something about my brother?"

"She's been in no shape to say anything about anyone. I'm hoping she'll feel like telling me what caused her to have the breakdown. Do you have any idea what it could be? It would help her a lot if you could tell me something or tell the doctor. She needs all the help she can get."

'She sure does. I told you she's crazy. Pay no attention to anything she says. She thinks my brother and his wife don't like her, but she hasn't tried to be friendly with them."

"Why would she think they don't like her? The four of you do things together, don't you?"

"Naw. We have more fun without her old sour face and straight-laced ways."

"Is that so? Don't you try to get her to participate with all of you in visits or trips together -- maybe a dinner together at each other's house?"

"I gotta go. I don't know what you're trying to prove or find out by pretending to be friendly with me. Just make sure you pay no attention to Lisa's crazy talk."

Willfred jumped in his car and drove off. Micah was frustrated. He felt that he got some information from Willfred, but not near what he needed. He made up his mind to try again. Maybe some time when his brother was in town he could talk to them both.

Lisa was well enough to go home, but she didn't want to go. "My daughter, Alena, is staying with a cousin and she doesn't mind staying there. My cousin wants her to stay. None of the family cares for Willfred. It took me a long time to open my eyes and discover why."

Dr. Ford was talking to Lisa in the solarium. He was pleased with her progress, but realized that the core of her troubles had not been recognized, at least not by her.

"Mrs. Kennedy --"

"Please call me Lisa."

"My pleasure. Lisa, are you prepared to tell me why you have been so stressed and worried? You've kept it to yourself so long that the brain decided to take a rest and not let you be bothered." He smiled at her.

"I don't really know what to tell you. I've discussed some of it with Sheriff Fleming, but not all of it. As I told him, I don't have absolute proof of my worries, just suspicions. I can't do anything until I know for a fact that what I'm suspecting is the truth. It would hurt too many people if I'm not sure."

"If you're not sure then it's wise to wait until you have proof."

Lisa's cousin, Eilenna Newcastle, with whom Alena was staying, offered Lisa sanctuary to complete her rehab. She had put obvious facts together and came to the conclusion that Lisa might be in danger. Eilenna felt that Willfred had shown no concern for Lisa or his daughters. Instead he had been argumentative and uncooperative. Her husband, Morris, had heard Willfred calling Lisa crazy and other derogatory names.

A week later Micah was elated to see Willfred and his brother, Orville in town with a young man of early twenties. He parked his car and sauntered along the sidewalk as if he were just taking a stroll. He finally caught up with them.

"Hey. Hello. How nice to see you gentlemen. Isn't this wonderful weather we're having, but the news promises thunderstorms tonight. Hopefully we'll all be inside and out of that."

Orville grinned at him. "Yeah, we need the rain though and I'm not complaining. Hey Sheriff, have you met my son, Porter?"

Micah reached to shake his hand. "No, I've not had the pleasure of meeting Porter, but I've heard a lot about you."

Porter looked startled and reluctantly shook hands. "You've heard of me. How?"

"I don't remember at this moment, but I'm glad to meet you."

Willfred barged in. "Did my crazy wife mention him to you?"

"Mr. Kennedy, in the first place your wife is not crazy. She was very sick and under a lot of pressure which was disturbing to her. I would love to know what caused her to become so upset. Do either of you have an idea?"

All three men just stared at Micah. Porter shrugged his shoulders. "I wouldn't have any idea what caused her to go off like that. I'm not here that often so don't see much of her."

"I know you don't come here to Shickshinny often, but I seem to remember someone saying they saw you here some time back. Something about a speeding car." Micah said innocently.

"Speeding! Who would know me here that could judge how I was driving?"

"I don't know, Porter. I only know what I've been told. I'm sorry to hear that you and your daddy have such an unreasonable hatred of the Amish. Your Uncle Willfred tells me they have done nothing personally to you, but you still don't like them. Care to tell me why?"

Porter looked dumbfounded and said a few swear words. "I don't exactly hate them, but I don't have any love for them either. They don't fit in here and no one wants them."

"Really?" Micah acted surprised. "No one?" He stopped two business men who were walking by. "Abe Isaac and Levi Auspitz, just the men I would like to speak to for a minute."

"Sure Micah, what do you want?" Abe asked.

"I'd like to know how you feel about the Amish living here?"

Abe and Levi looked at each other. "We have nothing against them. In fact they are good customers and Jacob Startz has made some beautiful furniture for me," Levi said. "I'll never understand why some misguided people hate them just because of who they are. They take care of their own and are not a burden to any of us."

Abe spoke, "Yes, a good example is that sweet Charity Kime. She is only nineteen and is now a widow with a new little baby. She has been courageous and is working to support herself and make a life for her little boy. Adam was such a good neighbor and hard worker. I hope whoever the driver is that ran them off the road and killed Adam and his precious horse will suffer for it. Lawfully we can't do anything about it, but boy if the whole town finds who did this cowardly deed, we'll want to take care of him ourselves."

Another voice spoke up. "Sorry, I'm not part of this group, but I couldn't help hearing the topic of conversation." Paul Meredith, President of the local bank was standing beside them. "I've had some dealing with the Amish and know how honest, God-fearing and kind they are. I hope that driver is caught. Even if we never know who did it, we know he'll rot in hell."

Levi slapped Paul on the back. "Yes. The coward who drove that car needs to see how Charity is struggling to be independent and provide for herself and her little boy. She is only nineteen and is to be admired. We need more citizens like that."

Porter was seething. "Why do you say the driver was a coward? Maybe he didn't know he'd hit the buggy. Besides, maybe he thought he was doing all of you a favor to get rid of an Aim-esh."

"Get rid of them!!" Paul was shocked. "How can you say such a thing? It's obvious you're not a Christian or you wouldn't think like that."

Porter had started to walk away. He whirled around and before his daddy or his uncle could stop him he barreled up in Micah's and the other men's faces. "You sanctimonious hypocrites putting on a fake face pretending to embrace the Aim-esh when deep inside you hate them as much as I do. You should be thanking me instead of judging me."

"Porter, are you saying you killed Adam Kime?" Micah calmly asked.

"Porter! You idiot. Don't say anything else. You're giving these people the wrong impression." Orville yelled at him.

Willfred reached to grab Porter's arm. "Come on boy before you let that slippery tongue get you in trouble."

What they didn't know was Micah had called for back-up when he first saw them on the street. At a nod of his head three deputies ran in and placed handcuffs on all three.

"I'm arresting you for the murder of Adam Kime and destroying valuable property. A little boy will never know his father and a young woman, not much more than a little girl, has lost a husband that she adored. She might be young but she is showing more maturity than you'll ever have. Take them away boys and book them."

Willfred was leaving yelling at the top of his lungs. "You're as crazy as that wife of mine. I'll sue you, I'll sue the county and you'll all be sorry."

Orville just hung his head and plodded quietly along.

Micah gave a deep sigh. Paul was elated. "Good for you, Micah. I told everyone you'd find the answer to the mystery of Adam's death. Maybe this will serve as a warning to others who might want to do the same thing."

"Don't celebrate yet. I don't have the proof I need and a slick attorney can still get them off free and clear. I have to get busy now and find the one thing I will need to make murder stick."

The three men did hire attorneys and were out on bail. Micah racked his brain until he had a headache. One day he was sitting at his desk and suddenly jumped up shouting, "That's it."

"What's it?" Several deputies gathered around.

"I'll tell you when I have the proof I hope to find. Glenn, I'll be out of town for a day or so. You're in charge until I return. Ellen," he turned to the secretary, "notify the Mayor that I've left town searching for evidence I need and I'll return in a day or two. Don't let anyone else know I've gone."

He ran home to pack an overnight bag and tell his wife where he would be. He drove to Wilkes Barre and checked into the Days Inn, 760 Kidder St. He called Anita to tell him where he was and then called Glenn. He went to a few auto repair shops that were nearby, but had to stop for supper and sleep.

Early the next morning he was up, had a quick breakfast and started hunting again. He began to feel discouraged and was afraid he had a bad idea. He decided that this would be the last auto shop and then he'd go home even though he felt like a failure.

He parked in front and went into the Avondale Auto Repair, 531 North Pennsylvania Ave. An elderly woman greeted him from behind a tall oak desk that almost hid her. She welcomed him and asked how she could help.

"I need to ask about a repair that was made either on 22nd or 23rd of September of last year."

"Oh, my. That's a long time ago. I'll call my son and maybe he can help you." She went to a door between the office and repair shop. "David, come here, please."

"Ma, I'm busy."

"This is very important or I wouldn't bother you. Sheriff Fleming is here and needs to talk to you."

"Whoa, boss. What have you done?" One man called as the others made remarks.

David came in wiping the grease from his hands. His coveralls were dirty from working under cars. "Hello, Sheriff, how can I help you?"

"I know this is a strange request, but I'm trying to find evidence in a murder case which occurred last September 22nd. I'm trying to find if a dark blue Cadillac sedan was brought in with a scrape on the right side. It might have left black or just took the paint off."

David thought and shook his head. "Sorry. Nothing comes to mind."

Micah tried one more time. "Do you know Porter Kennedy or his father, Orville? Do you ever do any work on their cars?"

David thought a moment and snapped his fingers. "Ma, find Porter's record on the computer. If that date is in there, then I'll have it in a hard file."

David and his mother looked at Porter's record. "Here it is," his mother said excitedly. David read the report and then went to a filing cabinet. He brought out a folder and sat at a table, nodding his head to show Micah to join him. "Yes, it's here."

"May I read what you have? If it's pertinent, I'll need a copy for the court files." Micah getting more excited as he read.

"The right front fender had a slight dent and a slash of black was running from that. The clincher is the blood found on the right rear tire." Micah slammed the folder shut saying, "Thank, you, Lord." He jumped up. "Thank you, folks, from the bottom of my heart. A twenty-one year old Amish husband was killed that night as was his horse. His nineteen year old wife gave birth to a little boy that night and the baby will never know his father."

David's mother wiped her eyes while David looked stricken. "Are you saying that Porter killed that young man?"

"I don't know. I don't know who was driving the car. I've been suspicious, but had nothing to go on. Now I must ask you both something that will be difficult to do. Please,

please don't talk about this to anyone other than us three. I don't want to alert people to run and hide or do something to cover evidence."

David and his mother promised that they would keep quiet. "I'll just tell my men you wanted to ask about car repairs."

Micah thankfully checked out and headed home. A soft rain had started spitting on the highway. He was singing to himself when a gun shot came through the windshield. "Holy creeps. Who can be doing that? Did someone follow me or did someone just happen on to what I was doing?"

He carefully controlled his car to keep the tires from spinning on the fairly wet pavement. A siren went screaming by him and he recognized a Pennsylvania State Police auto.

He saw the police car, almost a half mile ahead of him, pulling someone over. The driver did not want to pull over so the police car bumped the side of the sedan and forced it off the road. They stopped. Micah came behind them and pulled over. He stopped and cut his engine. Reaching for his hat, he exited his car and went to see what the police was doing.

"Orville Kennedy!" Micah was astonished. "Officer, this man is out on bail. He was arrested for suspicion of murder."

"Sorry to meet you this way Sheriff, "State Police Jake Wickham said. "I saw this man point a gun out his window and saw the flash as it fired. I pulled him over to determine why he was shooting and at whom."

"Look at the bullet hole and spider cracks in my windshield. He was shooting at me. How did he know I was in this area? I came to put together some evidence I needed to place his son at the scene of a murder."

"Hello. This just adds to your evidence. If he had not been guilty, he would not have fired on you. I'll have to arrest him and keep him here until I can take him before a judge."

Micah groaned. "That means I'll have to return to witness against him and then take him back to Shickshinny for a trial."

"Looks that way. Let's get out of this rain, Sheriff. I hope you get home safely. I'll send someone back to pick up his car."

Micah was glad to be headed home at last. He was very tired and frustrated. He wanted to get home to Anita whose pregnancy was causing joint pains, swelling and she had been nauseous the entire time. He kept thinking to himself. When are the two brothers and the son going to realize they can't win? Sure they can go free for several weeks, but justice triumphs.

CHAPTER SEVENTEEN

Wilkes-Barre is the county seat of Luzerne County, therefore all murder trials or trials of any importance had to be held in the county seat. Micah lived in Shickshinny and worked mostly from there, but he had to go to Wilkes-Barre.

Micah looked around the crowded courtroom thinking, half of Shickshinny must be here. Noticeably absent were the Amish. They did not approve of going to court unless they were ordered to be a witness or were accused of a crime.

The first few days were spent listening to evidence and determining if there should be a trial. There was no doubt. The next month had an open date for the purpose of choosing a jury. This took three days because men and women had to be chosen who would not be prejudice.

It was two months after the arrest before a trial started. In the meantime, Charity had her twentieth birthday, but wanted no fan fare. She just wanted to be quiet. Friends came by with gifts and her mother made a special cake and had the family in for dinner.

Jeremiah was now walking and often sitting down. He would just giggle and say "ups". He had heard the adults say, "Whups," when he sat down.

Charity would always love Adam, but was now learning to live with her grief.

Charity had talked to her daed about the fifty dollars that were left for Jeremiah. He said he would talk to the Bishop and decide. After much talking and thinking they decided that it could be placed in the bank for Jeremiah not to touch until he was old enough to handle it. There would be a lot of interest accumulated. At what age he could use the money was not agreed upon. The Bishop finally said leave it with the instructions that he could not use the money before twenty-one unless he got his mother's permission.

Charity had no desire to attend the trial, but the church leaders decided they would go and observe. They hired the Morrisons to take them in the car. Mr. Morrison stayed with them because he brought them home each night. He was interested because he knew Adam and Charity and felt they were the perfect example of a young marriage doing so well.

Judge George Donaldson was assigned to this case. He was known for going by the book and would not tolerate any courtroom shenanigans. The District Attorney, Andrew Miles, assigned his ADA (assistant district attorney), Ellen Bolling to work the case. She was known as a bulldog for facts and winning.

Willfred, Orville and Porter had all been advised to have their own attorney instead of one to represent all three. Manley Jessup represented Willfred; Ezekiel Marshall represented Orville and Henry Morgan represented Porter.

Bailiff Andrew Dallas has made sure everyone was checked for weapons before entering the courtroom. He now stood before the people and reminded them of courtroom rules and instructed them to absolutely not talk to any juror or to the judge. He checked to ensure that deputies were in locations where they might be needed.

Nine o'clock. The bailiff stood before the judge's bench and called, "Hear ye, hear ye. The court is now in session. Judge George Donaldson presiding. All rise."

Everyone stood as the Judge came in and took his seat. He had black hair thinning at the front with a sprinkling of white at the temples. His eyebrows were so thick and bushy that his dark brown eyes looked menacing. He could have been called interesting looking but never handsome. His six three frame was well padded and he looked as if he could hold his own if he were attacked.

Judge Donaldson struck the gavel saying, "Be seated. Before we start I want to remind everyone that there will be no talking or audible comments from the courtroom. If anyone chooses to break the rules, the bailiff, or a deputy, will escort that person out. If that person gives any trouble, I will order an arrest and hold you."

He then acknowledged each of the attorneys present and asked them if they were prepared to begin. All were.

Judge Donaldson instructed the bailiff to begin. Ellen Bolling stood and presented a skeleton of the facts of the case. Each of the defense attorneys had their turn. Ellen then stood and asked that Sheriff Micah Fleming be called. The bailiff nodded to a deputy who led Sheriff Fleming in from a room behind the judge. The bailiff swore him in and stepped back. Ellen Bolling stood and started her questions. It took two days to hear all of the sheriff's testimony. Then the defense attorney each tried to defend their own client and tried to cause the sheriff to appear to be prejudiced and having a personal anger toward these men. Of course his facts were not only true but could be proven.

Anita Fleming had wanted to attend but knew it would be too much stress so near her due date. Too, an ultra sound had shown twins. She and Micah were ecstatic.

The trial went on for three weeks. Everyone involved was exhausted. News reporters and television reporters were not permitted in the courtroom. They had reporters inside taking notes and feeding fresh news daily to them. The Amish church leaders were appalled when microphones were thrust in their faces and cameras were turned on them begging them to give their opinions. With no expressions on their faces, the Bishop just shook his head and they all walked in and out together.

Somehow reporters had sneaked a picture of Charity holding Jeremiah at the store. The story printed about her grief and courage brought tears to many eyes. Contributions started pouring in to help her. She was worried because first her image had been shown to the public and now money was coming in that was gained from the death of her beloved Adam. The Amish were taught from babyhood that money was not important. Hard work and a sense of self respect were more important.

Jacob advised Charity to use the money to do things Adam wanted done. The house was painted and gutters repaired. Fences were repaired and in some parts, replaced. She gave some to an Amish family who had a huge medical bill and very little money. She gave some to the church for the benevolent fund. Charity kept her ears and eyes open for a need that she might help. She didn't feel heroic or angelic, just grateful for her blessings and wanted to share.

Finally the trial was complete and it was now up to the jury to determine the outcome. After three days of being sequestered they found all three men guilty as charged.

Judge Donaldson read the suggestions of the jurors and after another month called everyone back to hear the verdict. The Amish had not attended every day, but did come on this day. The judge asked the three men to stand. The attorney stood beside each one. There was a strange silence in the courtroom.

Judge Donaldson looked the men sternly and spoke. "Porter Kennedy."

Porter and his attorney stepped forward. Lisa and Alena were in the courtroom and Lisa was quietly crying.

"Porter Kennedy, it was bad enough that you deliberately ran the buggy off the road causing the death of one Adam Kime and the horse. Mrs. Kime was taken to the hospital where she bore a small son in grief. She has no husband and the boy has no father. If you had come forward and confessed, it would have gone easier on you. Porter Kennedy, I sentence you to life in prison without parole. May God have mercy on your soul."

Orville's wife who was Porter's mother burst into loud sobs and had to be led from the courtroom. A deputy escorted Porter to a back room where his parents would have a chance to say good bye.

"Orville Kennedy." He stepped forward with his attorney. "Sir, you not only broke several laws, but you taught and encouraged your son to do the same. If you had helped him confess soon after the accident and then had done no more harm to innocent people, you would not be standing here. You also attempted murder on Sheriff Fleming, hoping to keep him from exposing your son and you. I' m sentencing you to thirty years in prison.

You may make an appeal, but I hope you'll take your sentence like the man you should have been. Tell yourself that you've learned from this and will, from this day forward, make a gallant effort to steer young people in the right direction." Orville was taken by a deputy to a back room.

"Willfred Kennedy." Willfred stepped up with his attorney. Lisa and Alena were in the courtroom. Lisa was sobbing out loud. "Sir, I'm astonished and sickened at you. With an excellent education, a loving family, a prosperous business and people who looked up to you, it was your decision to encourage your brother and nephew in their nefarious activities. I've heard no evidence that you've been directly involved in the crimes, you continued to support the ones breaking the law. You encouraged your own son which resulted in his death. I sentence you to fifteen years and hope you will use the time to change your attitude and live as a decent human being after this." A deputy led Willfred out.

There was absolute silence and then the courtroom broke into loud applause. Relieved sighs could be heard all over the room. When Judge Donaldson looked at the Amish he saw only quiet men who looked sad. He knew that deep in their hearts they were praying for the criminals and would not have any joy over the outcome of the trial.

When told the news, Charity just bowed her head and said a prayer. She had no hatred toward the men or cared for vengeance. She had been taught to leave all that to God and she believed it.

Anita Fleming came to the store one day with Lisa Kennedy. "Charity, Lisa wanted to come but didn't know how you would feel about her. She is hurt because of her husband's participation in the death of your husband. Not that he did it, but he knew who did and would not tell the sheriff."

Charity said nothing but came from behind the counter, walked to Lisa and hugged her. "You are a good, loving lady and I feel blessed to call you friend." Lisa was overcome with relief and tender feelings.

"Oh, Charity, I'm truly sorry about the loss of your husband and the cover up and I'm so ashamed for the breakdown when I interrupted your church service. In my poor sick mind, I guess I knew the right people to come to."

"It is already forgotten. Adam would be ashamed of me if I held it in my mind and in my heart. If he were here we would pray together and then forget it."

"I know and I'm striving hard to be more like that." Lisa sniffed.

They visited for a short time and Lisa told Charity to call her if she needed a baby sitter or a help in any way. Anita bought some honey, eggs, butter and a loaf of Charity's bread. They left promising to return.

As they walked out of the door of the store Anita gasped and doubled over. Lisa grabbed her before she could fall and Charity ran to help. Lisa called for an ambulance and Anita was rushed to the hospital. Maeve ran to the sheriff's office to tell Micah. He arrived at the hospital just in time to welcome Adam and Annalese to the world. The proud parents introduced them to the world the next day. The doctor explained that they had been carried long enough in the womb to be strong and healthy.

Micah and Anita were so well liked that gifts of all kinds poured in.

That night Deborah and Matthew took care of Jeremiah so that Charity could take a walk. They were staying with her for awhile. As she left the house she turned around to say, "Outen the lights. I'll get to bed. Danki."

Charity walked out across the pasture enjoying the fresh air and looking up at the sky full of beautiful stars. She stopped to try to locate constellations that Adam had taught her about. It was something he enjoyed. He read books about astronomy and remembered all that he learned.

While she was looking up she began to talk to Adam as she would when they walked together. She noticed one star seemed to be winking and imagined that it might be Adam telling her of his love for her.

"Adam, I'll always love you and I will tell our child about you so that he will love you as much as I do. Life is all right, but it was always better with you."

She told him all about the neighbors, what was going on at church and things she knew he would be interested in. She purposely did not talk about the trial and the men who had been involved in his death.

Turning to walk back to the house, she looked up again and saw the star winking. She smiled and blew it a kiss. "Gut nacht mine lieb."

Some Tasty Treats to Enjoy from Sioux Dallas

When baking, NEVER mix all ingredients together at once; add one at a time and mix well.

Springerle Cookies

4 eggs
2 tablespoons margarine (butter if you choose)
2 cups white sugar
4 cups all purpose flour
2 teaspoons baking powder
One fourth teaspoon salt
One fourth cup of anise seeds

Preheat oven to 350 degrees. Beat eggs, add margarine and sugar - cream together. Sift flour, baking powder and salt together. Add slowly to the egg mixture and combine. Knead dough until smooth. Cover and chill in refrigerator for at least two hours. Place on floured board press to one half inch thick. If you don't have a board, use a large sheet of aluminum foil. It's lovely if you have a roller with designs cut into it to transfer to the rolled dough. Sprinkle the anise seed on a clean tea towel. Place cut cookies on the anise seed. Allow it to stand overnight uncovered. Carefully pick up cookies with anise seed. Bake for about fifteen minutes at 325 degrees. Remove from oven and cool. Store in airtight container.

Rinderrouladen

Serves 4
4 flank steaks not more than 6 oz. each
One and one half cups beef broth
2 teaspoons Dijon mustard
One half teaspoon salt
One fourth teaspoon ground black pepper
2 sweet pickles sliced in strips
2 slices bacon
2 sweet onion chopped
One fourth cup vegetable oil
4 peppercorns
One half bay leaf
2 tablespoon cornstarch

Spread the mustard on each steak; sprinkle with salt and pepper. Place the bacon, pickles and onion across the top of the steaks. Heat beef broth and set it aside. Roll each steak like a burrito and secure with toothpick. Heat oil in heavy pan; add steak rolls and brown on both sides. Pour in hot beef broth, peppercorns and bay leaf. Cover and <u>SIMMER</u> for about one hour and twenty minutes. Remove steak and drain.

In bowl blend cornstarch with about three fourths cup cold water and mix well. (I use a fork) Stir into pan and bring to a boil until thick and bubbling. Pour over steaks and serve immediately.

Amish Whoopie Pie Cookies

1 cup shortening
2 cups sugar
1 cup very hot water with 2 teaspoons baking soda
Four and one half cups flour
4 eggs
Three fourths cup cocoa
1 cup sour milk
2 teaspoons vanilla
Pinch of salt

FILLING
1 cup milk
1 cup shortening
4 tablespoons flour
1 teaspoon vanilla
1 cup sugar

Mix cookie ingredients together. Batter is slightly thick so it can be dropped from a teaspoon. Drop onto ungreased cookie sheet into small rounds as much alike as possible. Bake at 375 degrees for 8 - 10 minutes.

For the filling, cook together the milk and flour until thick. Place in a bowl and add sugar, shortening and vanilla. Beat until spread able. Choose two cookies the same size and place the filling between them.

Friendship Bread Starter

1 cup white sugar
1 cup sweet milk
1 cup unbleached white flour

Combine the three ingredients in a large, non metal bowl. Stir with a non metal spoon. Cover with saran wrap but DO NOT refrigerate. Keep at room temperature. Stir the mixture carefully every day for 17 days. On the 18th day let it stand untouched. On days 19, 20 and 21 stir every day again. On day 22 stir and carefully add 1 cup sugar, 1 cup milk and 1 cup unbleached white flour. On days 23, 24, 25 and 26 stir each day again. On day 27 add a cup of white sugar, 1 cup milk and 1 cup unbleached white flour. Stir well. Keep a starter cup for yourself and give 2 friends each a starter cup.

TO KEEP THE STARTER GOING:
Do not refrigerate and do not use metal bowls or metal stirrer. Start on the 27th day again by adding twice as described above. On the 28th day keep another cup for yourself.

TO MAKE THE FRIENDSHIP BREAD:
Preheat over to 350 degrees
1 cup starter
2/3 cup vegetable oil
2 cups unbleached white flour
1 cup sugar
3 eggs

One and one half teaspoon baking powder
1 teaspoon cinnamon
One half teaspoon vanilla
One half teaspoon salt
One half teaspoon baking soda
1 full cup of raisins, chocolate chips, chopped nuts, dates and finely chopped apples.

Mix well in non metal bowl. Place in two greased baking pans. Bake at 350 degrees for 45 to 50 minutes. Cool before slicing. I like to eat a hot slice with a thin layer of butter.

MAKE SURE YOU KEPT A
STARTER CUP TO DO AGAIN.

Amish Walnut Kisses

1 pound shelled walnuts
2 cups granulated sugar
5 tablespoons all purpose flour
6 egg whites
1 teaspoon vanilla extract

Beat egg whites until stiff but not dry. Gradually add sugar and continue to beat until blended. Sift flour lightly over egg white mixture and fold in with a wire whisk. Blend in vanilla extract and nuts. Drop from teaspoon onto greased cookie sheet about 2 inches apart. Bake at 325 degrees for about 10 minutes. Yields 6 dozen small cookies.

Amish Yumazitti

8 oz. wide noodles cooked and drained
One and one half lbs. of ground beef (good grade)
One half cup diced celery
2 tablespoons butter
One fourth teaspoon pepper
Salt to taste
Ten and one half oz. can cream of chicken soup
Ten oz. can tomato paste
One half pound grated Cheddar cheese

Brown meat in butter and season with salt and pepper to taste. Place a layer of noodles in a 2 quart casserole, then one layer of meat. Mix soup, celery, and cheese. Place one layer of this. Repeat until all ingredients are used. Layer of cheese on top. Bake uncovered at 350 degrees for one hour.

Amish Homemade Bologna

3 lbs. good grade hamburger
3 tablespoons Morton's Tender Quick
1 cup water
One eighth teaspoon garlic powder
One half teaspoon onion powder
One and one half teaspoon Liquid Smoke

Mix well. Roll into two rolls. Wrap in saran wrap and place in refrigerator 24 hours. Place on greased pan. Bake at 300 degrees for one hour turning meat once halfway through baking time. Slice and eat.

Shoofly Pie

MIX FOR CRUMBS (reserve ½ cup for topping):
2/3 cup dark brown sugar
1 tablespoon solid shortening
1 cup flour

FILLING:
1 cup good, thick molasses
Three fourths cup boiling water
1 egg beaten
1 teaspoon baking soda

Combine hot water and baking soda, add egg and molasses. Add crumb mixture (minus ½ cup). This will be lumpy. Pour into unbaked pie crust and top with reserved crumbs Bake at 375 degrees for 10 minutes. Reduce heat to 350 degrees and bake an additional 45 minutes. When cut the bottom may be wet.

Amish Bread Pudding

2 cups scalded milk
One fourth cup butter
2 eggs
One half cup granulated sugar
One fourth teaspoon salt
1 teaspoon ground nutmeg
3 cups soft bread small pieces
One half cup raisins

Combine milk and butter over low heat until butter is melted. Combine eggs, sugar, salt and nutmeg. Beat at medium speed for one minute. Slowly add milk mixture. Place bread in lightly greased casserole. Sprinkle with raisins. Pour batter over all. Bake at 350 degrees for 50 minutes or until set. Can be served with lemon sauce.

Amish Cornbread

1 cup yellow cornmeal
1 cup flour
4 tablespoons sugar (optional)
1 teaspoon salt
4 teaspoons baking powder
1 egg beaten
1 cup milk
2 tablespoons melted shortening

Grease a baking pan. Preheat oven at 400 degrees. Mix cornmeal, flour, sugar, salt and baking powder. Make a well in the center and add egg, milk and melted shortening. Beat until ingredients are thoroughly mixed and not lumpy. Pour batter into pan and bake until risen and golden brown.
May add grated cheese on top if desired.
May use can of drained corn if desired.

Amish Buttermilk Pie

1 unbaked pie shell
One and one half cups sugar
One fourth cup flour
1 stick of butter (or margarine)
3 eggs
One half cup thick buttermilk
1 teaspoon vanilla

Mix sugar and flour and then add melted butter. Cream together. Add eggs, buttermilk and vanilla. Mix well and pour into pie shell. Bake at 350 degrees for 45 minutes or until knife comes out clean.

Amish Friendship Salad

1 cup small diced ham
2 cups cooked macaroni
One and one half tablespoon barbecue sauce
One fourth cup of grated pepper
Salt and pepper to taste
One fourth cup finely chopped onion
3 tablespoons mayonnaise
Three fourth cup grated celery
1 teaspoon prepared mustard
One half cup finely chopped carrots

In one bowl combine ham, macaroni, celery, carrots, pepper and onion. In another bowl mix mayonnaise, barbecue sauce and mustard. Mix thoroughly and combine the two.

AUTHOR'S NOTE

Hello Dear Readers,

I have chosen the Amish for this book because I have learned to admire them and respect them for their strong love of God and family. (I hope you saw the TV movie "Amish Grace") I visited them many times in Pennsylvania and was warmly welcomed each time.

Amish is pronounced ah - mish. While I was teaching public school I often took my students from Virginia to Pennsylvania to visit the Amish. Twice we were served authentic Amish meals.

Shickshinny was chosen for the setting because I was intrigued by the name. I found it means fine stream in the Native American language. There are many delightful names in the state that are interesting. I also found that Pennsylvania has more covered bridges than any other state.

Although people came to this area from the early 1600s the first permanent settler in Shickshinny was Ralph Austin in 1782.

Historians consider the Amish to be conservative Protestants. The majority of Amish consider themselves to be Anabaptist Protestants.

A large group was interested in the Protestant Reformation and during the late 1400s started forming their own groups. In 1525 in Zurich Switzerland a group outraged religious authorities by baptizing adults who professed to believe in Jesus and the Bible and promised to live by it. The baptism of adults was considered a crime and was punishable by death. This group felt that baptism was only meaningful for adults who understood what was happening. Because they had been baptized as infants in the Catholic Church they were angrily called Anabaptists.

Anabaptist hunters soon stalked these people to kill them. The first martyr of this group was drowned in 1527. Thousands were burned at the stake starved in prisons, beaten to death or lost their heads to the executioner's sword, all by the order of the Catholic Church. The MARTYRS MIRROR was published in 1660 in Dutch and today the German edition is found in many homes in Germany. This newspaper reports on the treatment of the Amish. The Swiss Anabaptists bravely tried to follow the teachings of Jesus in their daily lives by loving their enemies forgiving insults, turning the other cheek, being nonviolent and living peacefully. Although some became frightened for their families and asked for forgiveness and went back to their old ways their faith was tested daily.

The sting of persecution became too much to bear so some decided to make a life in another country. Some fled to northern France. Others went to Germany and the Netherlands. Along with the Amish are the Mennonites Brethren and Quakers.

The beliefs and practices of the Amish were based on the ideas of the founder of the Mennonite faith a Dutch priest Menno Simons 1496 - 1561.

When the Mennonites diversified due to differences of worship the group known as Amish led by Jack Amman in 1693 lived in Switzerland and around the Rhine River. They felt there was a lack of discipline among the Mennonites. The Amman followers were from Switzerland, France Netherlands and some parts of Germany. In the late 1600s and early 1700s a group of the people came to Pennsylvania from the Netherlands and were called Amish Dutch even though most of them spoke a form of German.

Amman proposed holding communion twice a year (at the beginning of planting crops in the (fruhling) Spring and after the harvest in the (herbst) Fall. He taught that they should follow the practices of Christ and wash each others' feet. (The washing of feet was done in Jesus' time because everyone walked on dusty ground and wore sandals. It was a common courtesy to wash a visitor's feet when they entered your home.) Amman saw it as humbling oneself. Amman developed a form of clothing that was plain and would not cause a person to be vain or worldly. He began the shunning of members being strict in rules and orders they were to follow.

Their education only goes through the eighth grade. Recently a Bishop has given permission for higher education if a youth wants to become a doctor, nurse, lawyer or veterinarian. They must prove they can make good grades and promise to work in their home area upon graduation.

These people did and to this day follow the practices of being slow to anger, passive about quarrels or fighting, faithfully following the Ten Commandments and working hard until they are too old or infirm to work.

A member of the family then builds an addition to their house so the older people can be independent yet close to be cared for. The Amish grow or make the majority of items or food they use and shun the world. They follow the same saying that we are supposed to go by: Be in the world but not of the world. They do not use anything that would place them in contact with the world such as telephones, electricity, cars, electrical appliances etc.

The Bishop gives those in business permission to have a phone either only for business or one in a shed outside the place of business for anyone to use only in an emergency. Air compressors are used in businesses that might require electricity such as a big sewing machine for cutting and making leather goods. Diesel engines are used in barns for the milking machines.

Propane or kerosene stoves are permitted in the house. Horse and buggy are used with no paint or gilt or anything that would draw attention or make a person feel proud or worldly. A member can ride in the car of an Englisch (English - those not of the Amish faith) in emergencies such as doctors appointments at a distance away or to and from the hospital. They can also pay an English neighbor to take them to and from the bus or train or visiting in another city.

Youth are not permitted to date until they are sixteen. Then they'll have permission to attend singings with other youth. The boys will "court" or ask the girl to allow him to take them home. There is no kissing or close contact.

There is no real dating such as youth outside the Amish do. At seventeen and sometimes older they have a year of Rumspringa which is a time to "sow their oats". They might experiment with drinking, smoking going to movies, learning to drive a car, dress in non Amish clothes or do things not allowed in the Amish faith. Sometimes a few will go together and rent an apartment in town to see if they'd rather live as Englisch. They then have a choice of living outside the Amish community giving up family and Amish friends or adhering to the Amish rules and faith and being baptized.

When they choose the Amish faith they'll then be baptized in the church and promise to follow the rules and regulations of the church.

When girls are eighteen and boys are twenty (or younger or older) they might choose a partner for life. They choose carefully for it is for life; no divorce.

Clothing is plain without buttons, designs in the material or anything that would make a person feel vain or better than others. The men wear plain black suits with no zipper in the pants, shirts with no collars or adornments, and suspenders. Clothing is usually held together with hooks and eyes. For men a straw hat is worn during hot weather and a black felt hat is worn during colder weather. Sometimes the men are permitted instead of a coat to wear a plain black vest. Black shoes or boots are worn the year around. 1 Timothy 2:9 gives them a guide of dress. Women must dress modestly with decency and propriety not with braided hair or gold or pearls or expensive clothes. Paul had given these instructions to people of Ephesus where Timothy led a church. Of course the men dressed the same with humble plain clothing.

Women wear long dresses, long black stockings, black shoes, and a white prayer kapp (cap). Their hair is parted in the middle, drawn back and put in a bun in the back with the white prayer kapp covering the head. Black bonnets are worn over the prayer kapp when they go outside their residence.

Sometimes a cape is worn. A new order of Amish can use different colors, lilac or green cloth for them to use to make their dresses. They can wear these as long as they do not use anything to make them "showy". No cosmetics or jewelry. They may wear white in which to be buried or the women can be buried in their wedding dress.

Farms have always been the major form of income. Lots of children are needed to work the farm and care for the animals. The women all have vegetable gardens and lots of flowers. Chickens, turkeys and peacocks are raised for eggs and meat and feathers; goats for milk cows for milk and some pigs are raised. The Bishops have given permission for members to have stores to sell to their own people as well as the Englisch.

Harness shops, shops that make buggies and farm wagons, gift shops which include the beautiful quilts that are handmade, house painters, garden shops with home-grown flowers, restaurants and to be helpers to veterinarians are permitted. The stores also sell items made by hand such as bird houses, dog houses, wooden containers to hold garbage cans and kitchen supplies such as wooden spoons, bowls, quilting frames and delicious bread, cakes, cookies and pies. A few women make quilts and clothing for sale and the faceless dolls.

Little girls have dolls made from stuffed cloth and dressed as Amish with no faces because that would appear to be worldly. They follow the Bible command of "No graven images" thus refusing to have their pictures made for fear of having a graven image. Too they don't want to have something that would make them feel proud or draw attention to themselves.

The younger people or the ones who have not yet joined the church can allow their picture to be taken as long as they don't pose and act worldly.

Church members, married people and older ones do not allow their faces to be seen in a picture.

I have been asked the difference among the Amish, Mennonite and Quakers. The Amish men grow a beard when they marry. (Following the instructions in Leviticus 19:27) The Mennonites and Quakers are clean shaven. The Amish live strongly by no worldly conveniences but the others will buy a black car with no chrome or trim or have a black telephone.

The Amish still shun a member who disobeys the rules or who lives among, or marries outside the faith. The Mennonite and Quaker do not believe in shunning. All of them reject violence and quarreling.